PURE
SLUSH
BOOKS

WILD

a collection

GILL HOFFS

Wild: a collection (second edition)
published by Pure Slush, October 2014

First published in paperback June 2012

Pure Slush Books
4 Warburton Street
Magill SA 5072
Australia

Find *Pure Slush* at http://pureslush.webs.com

Copies of all *Pure Slush* publications can be bought
at http://pureslush.webs.com/store.htm

All queries re *Pure Slush* can be made
via email to edpureslush@live.com.au

Dedication

For

the staff of Borders, Warrington,
where we spent such happy hours
amongst the books and muffins,
and won coffee mugs
and oddities as Team Fossil
in the quiz

and also

Matt and Jeremy

without whose help and support
this collection
would not have happened

Contents

Non−fiction

Acknowledgements

Foreword

by Jeremy Scott

I published my first book, a thriller, with Simon and Schuster in 1980. My latest title, *The Irresistible Mr Wrong*, came out in June 2012.

In the course of these 32 years and eight intervening titles, I have received over 100 letters from aspirant writers, asking advice on publication and enclosing samples of their work.

I replied to every one of them. It is only good manners to do so and to encourage the creative urge. Some of these samples showed talent, others not.

But in those three plus decades I never read one that startled and excited me so much I wanted to become *involved*.

Until September 2011 when Gill Hoffs sent me the first chapter and outline for her novel *An Unusual Darkness*.

I found it so singular in imagination and tone that the concept haunted me for days.

As a writer she has that rare ability to create a world, an atmosphere the reader is obliged to inhabit. She beguiles you, sucks you in… then deeply unsettles you.

Today, along with my own projects, I am working as Gill's editor on *An Unusual Darkness*. This will be a thriller that exceeds its genre and I found the job as its editor quite impossible to turn down.

Jeremy Scott is the author of *Show Me a Hero, Dancing on Ice* and the best–selling memoir, *Fast and Louche*. He lives in London.

FICTION

Firework sand

When the sand puffs at my heels as if the shore itself is spitting at me, when the crystals catch the light in a tiny galaxy of stars, sometimes close enough to sting the skin, that's firework sand. The tsunami took his hearing, left blood trickling from his ears long after the water drew back, but I can hear them. I can hear the deathly cracks.

There's a seagull wreathed in seaweed, green fronds fondling it in the shallows, and I must get it, I must, if we are to eat tonight. Sometimes cows wash up, bloated with the stinking sighs only the dead can hear. Once there was a giant squid, melting pearl and smelling of toilet cleaner, delivered by the waves. They took it back again, and the cows. We don't eat those, nor the pets or the bodies, but the fresh corpses, the new dead, we do. We have to. We must.

Kyle's so thin his fingernails look as though they've come from bigger fingers, maybe dad's. But I don't want to think about him, just now. Sneak… sneak… a suicide sneak, past the rocks and the barnacles and the fallen trees, over ropes and nets and bottles and buoys, under the beams and rafters of a roof wedged tight with exhaustion with boulders for walls. Is there anybody there? Are they watching? Are they peering through small circles of sights, taking aim, ready to fire?

They blame us.

He's five and I'm ten and they blame us.

It's not long dead, caught in some netting, drowned I think.

When I lift its sopping weight from the waves, the netting comes too, and there's a lot of it. It's heavy, too heavy, and I can't break the mesh, daren't use my teeth. Instead I pull, turning to go, ready to dart left and right, port and starboard, up and down, to dodge the bullet and their blame.

If I'm lucky, if *we're* lucky, there'll be fish caught too, fresh ones with plenty of meat on them. I try not to think what they've been feasting on, somebody said we are all made of stars but as far as I can tell, we're all made of things eating other things, dead things, not just plants but names and faces. Maybe my pinky finger has a bit of Elvis somewhere, maybe my kidneys a little Cleopatra. Perhaps my nose was once a dolphin, my skin a dinosaur's tail. Mum and dad are probably whales right now; fish first, then whales, then something else, something wonderful and strong.

It's really dragging on the sand and I can't help but glance at the mountain side trees, at the deep dark green with the villagers within. Maybe there's no−one here today, maybe I'd be okay to wander and walk, to traipse and dawdle, write my name in the sand and sunbathe. More likely they want a clean shot, or for me to be higher up the shore, or west a bit, or standing, or sitting, or whatever the heck it is they think a ten year old girl, a *tourist* for goodness sake, should be doing as penance for their loss.

It's really heavy. I'm moving as fast and as secretly as possible, but the net's dragging on the sand. If it's got bodies, I'll leave it by the cave; the tide can do with it as it will, but if it's fish or *things*, good things, interesting things, helpful things, then by golly we'll sleep well tonight. Once there was somebody's suitcase on the shore, all packed and ready to go, maybe from the hotel by the harbour, no, that used to be by what was the harbour. We're still using the toothbrush and smearing the paste, like our folks taught us, like we did at home. Kyle sleeps in it at night; it's big enough, just. Curls up in a ball in a nest of old lady clothes, pinks and purples cosy in the darkness. I have a bed next to him of sand and seaweed that I clear daily, high up in the system of caves. It doesn't even smell bad anymore, not since I got rid of the stink. The stream trickling inside, rainwater from the island above, used to make me want to pee a lot, but now I barely notice it.

I want to look, oh boy do I want to, but I have to keep my eyes on the trees, watch out for a glint or a movement that means the sand will be spurting today. Kyle's at the entrance, I can feel him watching me, thumb in mouth, waiting for my safe return. He knows better than to call out, knows better than to come out onto the pale sugar sand; we used to be three.

Then they shot Lorna, and that was that. We were two.

Perhaps another two hundred yards to go. I'll need to avoid the outcrop and the wreckage, else the net might snag. It's heavy and I feel too exposed but now I'm on the drier sand it's not so slow.

Their superstitions work in our favour too. Not enough to make up for the shooting, the murder and the fear for our lives, but enough for us to find refuge in their sacred caves and not be hunted there, too. We found gold and a skeleton, an old one with busted legs. Kyle was thrilled, swaggering about pretending to be a pirate, 'aarr'−ing and playing with thick heavy coins. I was better pleased with the knife by its side, something to carve our meals with and protect us against those who would do us wrong. Kyle keeps it whenever I go.

Nearly there. A bit of sick, maybe only a spoonful though it feels like more, is burning at the back of my throat and I really *really* want to scream.

In, I throw myself in, and roll with Kyle on the sand, fizzing with the relief of being 'home'. The net can wait, now. We've made it, we're here.

Kyle helps me haul it in, he's strong for five, strong for starving, and I'm pleased. We climb up the rocky stairs within, rubble really but stepped just so. He's left the knife by the entrance and I let him keep pulling the net up as he stumbles towards the sky hole and the light when I too stumble. I see what he's dragging in.

She's beautiful, shivering and shiny, twinkling with her own tiny lights. Older than me, I think, but sheathed in the twisting twining mesh it's hard to tell. Her skin is the pale green of a bark–stripped sapling, her hair blacker than tar, and the lower half of her body is the rainbow'd silver of salmon. Plucking the knife from the sand by our entry hole, I run up the rugged steps to my brother and motion him to stop. He smiles, and I kiss his nose and pat his bum so he'll sit down, then scamper back down to our catch.

Could we eat her? She'd keep us going for weeks if I lay strips in the sunshine under the sky holes, drying fillets for jerky later. Was she more fish or more human, or neither... was she even edible?

If I was going to do it, I should do it now while she was out of it, unaware, unfeeling, defenceless. Where? Would her neck be best, her chest – I couldn't help but notice it was fuller than my mother's – or was it different with them?

No belly button. No fingernails. I didn't need to know how she poo'd.

Cutting the net instead, the plastic tough, its fibres splaying, I remembered how I used to pull the red netting apart with just my fingers when dad brought a bag of satsumas home from the market where he worked. Fruit... my mouth watered and I looked at the rounded green of her, swallowing, wondering.

She sat up and I could see the ocean in her eyes, smell the sweet salt of her breath, hear the rushing of the waves outside as they came to claim her. Froth swirled round her in a tickle of bubbles, pulling her beauty away, and her smile was the pinky pearl sheen of an empty shell. Salt water rushed down my face, another loss, the entrance emptying again and I stood to go to my brother, feet sinking into sand.

16

Then another wave, a gush of bounty. The cave filling as never before.

And I knew we wouldn't go hungry again.

Snow Go

My dad told me when I chose my little run—about that white was the worst of all colours.

"It'll show the dirt, Tina."

"I can clean it."

"Scuff easier than cheap shoes from the market."

"Not if I'm careful with it."

"You'll look like half the other cars on the road."

I put it down to some kind of generational racism, ignored him with a hug. He never told me it might kill me, but why on earth would he know?

I was driving home for Christmas, home to my mum's. A surprise, the best present I could give her in my current state, living off loose change and free doughnuts, waiting tables in the café near my digs. There was just enough petrol in my car to get me the fifty miles or so through the highlands to the coal fires of home; my Christmas present from her would be the fuel to reverse the journey.

We didn't get on, my mum and I; when I told her I'd lost weight, she asked if I was sure. When Benny asked me out, she wondered why. Things used to be better, before they split, but when I looked in the mirror I saw my dad with better hair. That couldn't be easy for her, but it definitely wasn't for me, not since the divorce and the push—me—pull—you of possessions between her and my dad. But with the chemo and all, and the café closed after the flood, I'd figured it might be wise to try for one last merry Christmas.

The drive was a slow one, the higher I drove the whiter the way. Thick slow flakes blew through the fuzzed sky, reminding me of the confetti thrown by mum's friends as my dad drank away the divorce in his local. Moving out of radio range, I switched the thing off as the static crackled on my nerves: just the steady pause and thump, pause and thump of the wipers clearing my view on the slowest setting kept me company.

The white dancing and swirling over the vanishing road was making me yawn, reminding me of the old insomniacs' cure of counting sheep. But no sheep here, the shepherds would have cleared their flocks from the highest peaks, brought them down for food and shelter. I drove past the pink stain of fresh road kill, my foot on the brake as I slowed and slid round the corner to the car park.

Though it was harder to tell in the blizzard, there was usually a cracking view from the far side, right across the valley to the North Sea. I parked beside the verge. Closing the car door with a thump, I was glad to get out in the fresh air.

The snow was crisp and crunched under my boots, and despite the nip in the air I kept my hands out my pockets in case I slipped and fell. I'd been here before, several times, so I knew there was a path under the soft duvet of snow and followed it round white hillocks, round as rolls in a baker's window, in case the view was better round there. The horizon was uncertain in the whirling snow, and the world was smaller, quieter, sleepier than before.

I was utterly alone. Out of sight. Out of touch. Free.

Glad of the breather, I smiled to myself. I sniffed, and wiped my nose on my hand, then my hand on my jeans. A snowplough grumbled, low, as it crested the pass behind me. I looked at my watch, considering. If I wanted time to talk to my mum before her boyfriend got home, I had to be there before six. It was nearly three now, dark delivered in half an hour.

Puffing warm breaths into the freezing air, I followed filling-in footprints back to my car. I used my sleeve to clear the windscreen; some of the flakes fell into the cuff and melted cool against my skin. Shaking what I could off my arm, I sighed: the sleeve would soon dry in the heat of the car.

The blizzard was turning the sky from pink to grey, the flakes thickening. I hopped in, started the engine with a wish and a splutter. Heater on and gusting, the car took a few seconds to grind out of the dips.

Reversing, I slid towards the exit, the wheels slipping on the snow but nothing I couldn't handle...

Oh no. Oh no no no.

That hadn't been a snowplough, or at least, if it was, it hadn't just been out ploughing snow. The solid metal of the barrier arm had been real enough through the swirl of ice.

The heavy silver padlock dangled, anything but Christmassy. I checked my phone, though I knew there was no point, really. No bars.

I looked up through the windscreen again. Yes, somebody had locked the car park.

No way out, no way round, no way through. No food, just water frozen white all around me.

The key was tiny in my hand as I turned it, locking the door. Tugging the zip on my coat as high as it would go, I shrank into the warmth of its folds as I abandoned the car.

Cold in my soul, I started walking.

Acceptance

It was raining when I found his glasses on the moor, a typical misting drizzle that chilled the skin and gathered on the wiry grass, but leaves a person reluctant to wear a hat or pull their hood up, because by the time the weather's apparent, hair and hood are already wet.

My fingers fumbled fine wire as I reset the snare. We would eat well tonight, and Mam would cuddle me, pleased with my pale brown haul for the pot. Something crunched under my denim—ed knee as I checked the warrens for fresh round droppings, grapeshot poo that would tell me whether to bother with this hole or find a new burrow. There was hardly a shortage in this desolate place, the only creatures I saw up here were rabbits and the occasional stray, white rimmed eyes searching for a route home, the car that dumped them probably back in Manchester or Leeds days before.

Curiosity moved my leg; nosiness dug the legs of the spectacles from under the ground. Clearing the undamaged lens with my pinkie, as usual the cleanest of my fingers, I tried them on. Whose nose had they pinched last? And when? All was a blur, and my forehead ached. I dropped them to the side, done with the experiment, and stood, rabbit dangling at my side, taking my bearings for home.

But someone was watching me. A small grey figure stood atop a hillock perhaps a quarter mile from where I held dinner by velvety ears. Not an adult, not any child I knew, or I'd have heard them before now. This morning's small death weighed lightly in my hand.

There was no hurry, Mam would be busy with Alicia, bathing her, nursing her, or cooing over the pale beauty, and I was too busy to bear witness to that. My eyes scanned the gentle roll of the moor, the slant of hill sometimes broken in this area by a misty braille of hillocks and tussocks where boulders had been abandoned by glaciers long ago, and seasonal streams cut away at the softer sections, ribboning brown veins through the short yellowed grass.

I felt no danger here, those that had haunted the moor, fertilising it with the unlucky and the unwilling, would not stand on this springy soil again. Locals that were left found other pastures for walking their dogs, riding their horses, or catching butterflies in ridiculous nets. For want of a better description, this was a shadowed place, as I imagined the Glencoe of school's textbooks, and if colours had odours, grey would smell of the moor, damp, bleak and foreboding.

The figure wisped closer, a silhouette seeking company. I stood my ground, waiting.

"What's that you found?"

I paused before answering the boy's question, wary of the friendly tone.

"Just some specs. Old ones."

He cocked his head to one side, as I'd seen crows do as they eyed their surroundings for competition, picking the eyes from flattened creatures on the road. I tilted my face back, slitting my eyes against the drizzle, preparing for the usual remarks about my skin, or the hair I felt frizzing along my neck. But he only replied:

"Want to see something *really* interesting?"

Traipsing along the tufted surface, peaty water swirling rainbows beside my boots more vivid than any I'd seen in the far off sky, I swung the furry body at my side. Companionship is a foreign concept to me, but silence is a second skin, so I followed behind, thinking of buried treasure and metal detectors, Saxon hoards, gold, glory. My mother proud, plaiting my tricky hair for the newspapers, relaxing with a shiny smile.

A person could walk the moors every day of their life, live to be a hundred, and still find themselves lost amongst a russet patch of bracken, or a hundred feet beneath grass, trapped in a disused shaft. Tin was mined here, copper too, Miss. Hennessy told us about it in a local history lecture. And the shafts await feet heavier than a rabbit to swallow the unwary whole. So I let him go yards ahead, his feet barely seeming to touch the grass, waterlogged earth refilling my footprints instantly.

Perhaps ten minutes passed, as we headed to the lower ground, not a tree in sight, but wizened gorse brightening my wide open nostrils with its coconut holiday scent, the dark green prickles masking its pale contorted structure, reminding me of a seasons dead hedgehog I saw after the snows. A rocky outcrop, lichened with peeling yellow and grey, jutted beside an overgrown hole, visible only from a certain angle. Curved shells lay in unfinished mosaic, smashed by a hungry thrush, buttermilk and brown, striped, or flecked white, and the grey child beckoned me closer.

"It's in here. Toward the back, you'll see."

Then I noticed his clothes, got a proper look at him. I had a nagging feeling I knew him from somewhere, not school, not to speak to, but somewhere. Grey v−neck, no sleeves, grey shirt, dark shorts with the hems fraying a fringe over his skinny white legs, knee−socks sloughing down towards his ankles, and a blinking unfocussed look on his friendly freckled face. Perhaps he hadn't noticed my skin, I thought. That could explain it.

"What's in there?"

His smile revealed splayed teeth, still finding their rightful place in his mouth. Moisture trickled down the back of my neck, and I shivered, the rabbit dancing by my leg.

"Something interesting. I think you'll like it."

The grass grew long and undisturbed at the entrance to the hole.

"Like what?"

The sky darkened further, a summer storm heading our way. A leaden curtain of rain appeared to prop up the purpling clouds crowning the higher ground to the left. Mam didn't allow me an umbrella, fearing its use as a weapon, attracting more trouble to our graffiti'd door.

He shrugged, still smiling.

"You'll see!"

Reckoning I outweighed him, and definitely out–toughed him, I tucked my unease away and carried on into the gloom. It took a moment for my eyes to adjust. Grit and sand crunched under my feet, and musty smells reminded me of the breadth of my nostrils, for it felt as if every inch was stinging with the stink of the place. Playground taunts filled my ears in the silence, memories of school–mates rushing to fill the hush, reminding me that if I close my eyes and mouth in the dark, no–one would know I was there. Useful for circumstances such as this, though I was uncertain of what exactly this situation was or could be.

I hadn't seen him duck the bindweed wreathing the entrance, or noticed the little light there was lessen as he moved beside me, but he had. We walked back and I realised this was a tunnel. Then we got to the back, and I reassessed: it was a tomb.

There was the creamy bowl of a skull, rags bundling nobbled sticks together, shrouding the clawed fingers of a ribcage in a grey shirt and sweater. There was nothing about the smell to make me heave, yet I felt the urge in the dusty air. Perhaps I would have, had Mam provided breakfast instead of offering a banana for me to go out on instead. Sometimes I wondered if she too meant to taunt me. For without the betrayal of my appearance, she'd pass.

24

"What do you think?"

"What do you mean?" Dinner's fur was cold in my hand. "How did you find it? Have you told anyone?"

He sniggered, an unsettling sound in the darkness of our situation.

"What?"

And now he laughed, too high for my liking, its unseemliness echoing off the walls. The fur was cold and damp now in my sweating palm.

"Nothing. Really, nothing." He took control of himself. "You're the first I've told. Why, what do you think?"

I yearned for the cleansing summer rain, and took a step toward the outside.

"I think we need to tell the police. What if someone's looking for them?"

Would my mam? If it was me?

"I think they've stopped now. If they ever did."

Another step. I moved slowly, though keen for air, so as not to frighten him, then wondered why. The boy seemed perfectly comfortable here. Perhaps overly so.

"What makes you say that?"

I felt the breeze of ill weather caressing my face.

"Sometimes I get lonely."

Puzzled, unnerved, I paused in my exit.

"Eh?"

He was there, at my side, between me and the light, only now I could see the substance of him. Or lack of it.

I ran through the cold, eyes tearing up, lips smarting, until I was far from the dumping of that unlucky boy. He didn't follow, and it felt like abandonment. Rain washed the dust from my curls, and the soil from my fingers, but no matter the fluid, no matter the soap, I could never clear the mud enough for my mother.

Home, I ran home, clenching the rabbit as talisman to normality. Alicia was having her nap, my mam asleep in the chair

25

by her cot. Her skin glowed palest caramel against the yellow cover, and she could have been twenty again.

In the kitchen—cum—living room, I cleared straightening irons from the counter before depositing dinner—to—be, fetching the skinning knife from the drawer by the sink, doing not thinking, while deep deep down, in the essence of me, something picked and pulled at the problem, offering an unpalatable solution.

No, I couldn't do that.

Really, I couldn't.

Could I?

The knife slipped, the tip sliced my finger at the crease, my blood mingling with that of the rabbit. I swore aloud.

Mam was on me in an instant, hissing her displeasure, cursing my clumsiness and lack of consideration for my sister.

"You could have woken her, and you know how hard it is to put her down. Really, you disappoint me at times."

It felt like all the time. Nursing my unchecked finger, sneaking toilet paper to it as bandage, I looked about with sorrowful eyes. Without Alicia, my mother would never have had the temptation to pass, but a golden child with strawberry blonde ringletted hair who drew coos of admiration in the street showed my mother exactly what she could have had. Without me, she still could.

But this was my home first, I thought, full of memories. The picker and puller of problems whispered, *yes, but think of these memories, think of the shame,* **think** *of school.* And think of the option. The escape.

After an ungrateful dinner, watching my mother bounce Alice on her knee, shining her smile but never at me, I went to my room. Tomorrow, I thought. See how I feel then.

After another banana breakfast, I watched my mother cutting stars and flowers in her daughter's buttered toast, as Alicia smeared eggs on her face.

I sorted things out and left, wiping their blood on a dishtowel.

At the corner shop I spent the gas money on matches, chocolate and loo roll, the other children made monkey noises as I made my choice.

The moor was pale green and glowing under the azure blue sky, swifts darting black after flies, brown butterflies fluttering low. I checked yesterday's snares, collected my catch and the spectacles. Then I was on my way, sometimes glimpsing grey movement from the corner of my eye.

Today I noticed the pale beauty of the bindweed flowers, the presence of a clear stream nearby, and the tranquillity of this spot. Inside, I let my eyes adjust, the smell less foreign to me now. Accepted in the dark, I moved to the reluctant remains, squatting on my haunches for a closer look. Placing the glasses round the skull, more gently than I had ever seen to my sister, I murmured a soft "hello".

And from behind me, my friend replied:

"Welcome home!"

The premature ending
of Annie Macleod

I was gutting mackerel when they came for me, my fingers dipping in and out of rainbow'd bellies, trailing pink as I cried for dad, and island life carried on. My mother, proper in mourning black, stuffed me under a pile of nets when she heard them riding along the shingle shore to our home. The sun trickled through in tiny diamonds. I lay there, listening to her lie over the *shhh* of the surf, smelling fresh fish and old twine, as a sneeze built in my head and the sorrow rose angry in her voice.

"What are you lot after now?"

"Your daughter hasn't attended school despite the warnings. You've had the letters, we've explained the procedures. It's time for her to go."

One of the horses was unsettled by something, perhaps my quiet struggles with the mounting pressure in my nose. It backed up and nearly stood on my leg beneath the nets. The rider clicked his tongue, urging it forward, annoyance in his voice.

"I've just lost Annie *and* her father – check your paperwork, you heartless toe–rags. Besides, we home–schooled. So you can just sod off back to the mainland. Now, if you please."

There was some murmuring, and I'm sure I heard the nearest of them say something about "nut–jobs". I held my breath and hoped either the sneeze would go or they would.

"We'll need to see the records and take copies before we can close this off, as I'm sure even you can appreciate. It's in your interest to show us them so we can go back to the boat. Like you want us to. We've no wish to intrude here. And, er… we're sorry for your loss."

He didn't sound it. Just impatient.

"Fine, if that's what it takes to get you off our island, so be it."

I heard the door of our croft scrape shut across the summer warmed flagstones, then one of the men offer my mother a ride on his mount. She spat on the path in answer, and a deep voice muttered something about "the bleeding dark ages". They clattered off slowly, along the beach path that wound behind our home, up through the blue hats of harebells and pink tufts of thrift dotting the coarse green of the island's west face. Our church hides within a ring of outbuildings, small and growing smaller with every winter wind and stone's fall.

My father kept it carefully, repairing what he could, securing the records and sacred silver in a great black trunk in its cellar. Away from my mother, when he dared. We rarely used them, instead worshiping with our deeds and purity, but it was nice just knowing they were there. He stored a secret box in the darkness, too, away from my mother and her friends, but we were close, he and I. So I knew of the wireless.

Then I worried–

What if they took it? What if they saw?

The sneeze fizzed through my nose and out with a sprinkling of spittle, but there was nothing to hear it now save the gulls whipping white through the sky, diving for the sunlit shore.

Though I knew it was forbidden, I followed the Mainlanders till I could see…

And there past the crosses, fresh and new, were the tethered horses. Lent by Bill at the jetty, for the day. Crawling through the yellow buds and dark prickles of gorse, their coconut smell sweet in the air, I snuck ever closer till at last I saw.

"Annie and John died a month ago, a fall from the cliffs. I'm no a numpty. The paperwork's all filled out, correct, witnessed by the Reverend himself, so you can take yourselves back to the boat now."

After the horses had cantered off to Bill and their hay—nets, the Mainlanders only having to hold on to return, I saw my mother walk not back to our home but over the field to her friends.

Sneaking into the cellar, I looked for the box, and wondered about dad falling like that. And mum's midnight walks. And that night on the beach.

But the wireless was gone.

And so was he.

I wondered...

The Rabbit and the Dam

I woke again to the smell of wet dog; a child's damp footprints glistening on the old wood floor. There were two sets, the wettest ones leading to my solitary single bed, those returning to the doorway nearly dry, disappearing before my bleary eyes.

Dressing in blouse, slacks and comfortable boots I rubbed sleep from my eyes, unlocked the door, and stumbled downstairs to join my fellow guests for breakfast. Passing the parlour door with still slumbering feet, I witnessed the landlady polishing and damn near caressing her television set with the pride of a new mother. Varnished veneer sparkled, the focus of the pale pink room. The grate lay cold and untended, ignored in the summer heat, chairs turned away in preparation for the Event. Flags stood drooping in the corners, propped in ugly vases and umbrella stands, scenting the room with mothballs and cedar from their post−war storage. As I watched, she dabbed the screen with a spit−wet finger; I sought refuge in food, ignoring inviting tureens of tinned tomatoes and almost−egg.

Today's Gazette predicted the drought would break over the next few days. I ate a breakfast of lumpy porridge as I read, the paper full of the new Queen's Coronation. It had been an article just two days ago that prompted my inevitable return, the headline "Village resurfaces after 7 years!"

§

It was the first time since the great flood that even the weather cock atop the manor house had felt valley air, let alone the rest of the village. But with thunderheads building in the east, I had perhaps the rest of today to find what I needed.

Bag packed and slung over my shoulder, I left my things on the bed and the key in the bedroom door. It was a forty minute walk down the hill from Penketh Lee through fragrant buzzing country lanes to reach the new shoreline. A 'No Entry' sign stood, casually ignored. The policeman who had stood sweating sentry in the summer heat for the past few days was now with all other available officers of the law, supporting the Coronation, quelling complaints from an anarchic few.

Flower laden hawthorn gave way to the skeletons of long drowned trees and hedges, browned fields and thick stinking mud. I followed the lane into the past, down the steep bank, my feet knowing the way almost without looking despite it being seven long years since I called this place home. There on the left was the old barn, thatch long gone, rafters darkly drying.

The village had huddled here, terrified, eleven years ago, during our closest encounter with the war. The bells of St. Elphin's had pealed long and loud, shocking us from our beds, sending us tearing in slippers along lanes and paths to windowless safety. The full moon lit our way and that of the German pilots on their way to bomb the dam holding its water high high above our heads. Servicemen home on leave, village lads and their friends, ushered us into the unnerving darkness. I had whimpered, a frightened young woman, and kind hands had led me to the hayloft away from the bedtime breath and murmurs of the crowd below.

Tabitha was not there.

My sobs attracted strong shoulders to cry on, smells of maleness and sweat. The straw prickled and itched against my thighs and back.

Comfort led to dark conception that noisy night.

The dull clanging of ropeless bells at St. Elphin's shook me from my reverie. Imagining our bright, young queen approaching Westminster, I carried on, round the corner, past the old Post Office cum village store, sign rusted brown but still intact. In the still hot air of this lonely Tuesday morning, it began to sway.

There on the right was the village pump, the trough underneath brimming with fetid water. The stench of rot and decay stung my throat, making me cough for cleaner air. With memories of thick winter ice alive in my mind, fingers remembering the sharp nip of grasping frosted metal, I continued along the dank street, sure I heard something small slithering from the water trough behind me. I felt no desire to look back.

A granite obelisk, paid for by local subscription – mainly Tabitha and her family – spiked the top end of the street, commemorating our sacrifice to the Great War. Amongst the mud–softened outlines of houses and pavements, it jutted like a black knife from the ground. My father's name was still darkly legible against the polished grey – we had never met; he perished in foreign dirt when a shell landed too close to his trench. It was his first day back from leave, having impregnated my mother in his last week home. I used to come and talk to the grim granite when I did well at school or felt unjustly chastised by my sickly mother. That spire was alien now.

I resisted the temptation to enter any of the derelict buildings, though I felt curiosity beckoning me in, and made my way toward Greystones Hall. The church had lost stained glass on three sides, the sun shining through marvellous arches, but one section remained intact, glowing with the blues and pinks of a weeping Mary, and her sorrowful son. It was as if their pain followed me as I walked on by, and I shivered in the sun.

Many of the gravestones in the churchyard had lain down as if to rest, carved crosses embracing plain tablets, basking in the light. At the far side of the graveyard, near the dry—stone wall which used to be cloaked with convolvulus every summer, stood the poor rabbit's gravestone. A pre—emptive epitaph for my only child, lost at birth. A tiny pink naked thing, wrapped in a pillowslip in the painfully small coffin.

I had stood, pale with the strain of separation and shame as the village turned out to mourn the loss of one of its children. The minister patted my arm, kept me strong, as I endured the glances and mutterings "poor dear, first her husband was missing, now this." "She'll have more, she'll soon forget." No, I bloody wouldn't. I silently wept as clods of earth thudded on cheap thin wood.

The 'cah cah' of crows was reminiscent of late autumn on this bright June day. Black and white flashed at the edges of my vision, too quick to focus on. Magpies, I lied. Here to breakfast on the dead fish left stranded in the filth. I continued past the abandoned church. To Greystones.

When Andrew died six years ago witnesses to the single car accident spoke of a dog. They thought it was a dog, only it was all so quick, they said. A terrible shock, not what one would expect in broad daylight, you see? A collie or something similar. The funny thing, one man said, was that it was sopping wet. Absolutely dripping. That had stuck in his head, for it was a hot summer's day in the middle of the high street, no water lay anywhere nearby. And the poor creature had moved strangely too. He had looked for it, suspecting it a stray and probably injured, but found no sign of it anywhere. The wet paw prints simply stopped at the other side of the road. No—one had reported a dog like that missing so they were very sorry ma'am, the police said, there was nothing they could do.

Widowhood suited me. To be frank, I had married young on its expectation. No hair bracelets or widow's weeds for me, a

34

quiet funeral, then swift relocation to a new flat away from things, furniture, and colour schemes chosen together.

And here was Tabitha's house, though to describe it so simply is akin to calling Hepburn pretty. Greystones Hall had sat, comfortably rich, on the northern side of Thorndale village like a sow suckling her litter. To the back of it had laid acres of fields, meadows, copses, and streams full of little brown trout. The few village streets had sprung from its front like rays from the setting sun, the old pump and stocks on cobbled streets either side of the main entry. Greystones Hall had survived the scurrying priests of Henry VIII's reformation, and to a certain extent had survived this tragedy, too. A long fallen tree held the wrought iron gate open.

Pausing at the stocks to take a bottle of ginger—beer from my bag, I popped the top, half—emptying it in several long swigs. Perhaps she was supping champagne now, steadying her nerves before her long walk along the carpet — or was it all over, and time for the guests to experiment with their new chicken dish and fancy forks? It was so easy to lose track of time, though each minute weighs heavily on me without them. Stifling the inevitable burp out of bred—in politeness, my eyes watered as it prickled my nose. I carried on up the driveway. Here Tabitha and I had 'dug for victory', uprooting her long dead mother's roses for hopeless re—potting and planting cauliflowers, carrots and onions, leeks and sprouts standing sentinel beside.

Swallows darted like bats in great arcs down to the mud and back, feasting on flies drawn to the decay. Tabitha once came squealing to the groundskeeper's cottage in which I lived with Jed, an aerial acrobat caught in her curly chestnut hair. An old pink towel quietened the bird while I extricated it as best I could, at last resorting to a strategic haircut to set it free. It had fluttered away in fright, soaring high into a wheeling black dot. Tabitha and I had watched it, the sun rosying her cheeks. I felt the smarting of sunburn on my nose but sat anyway, on the back step, ignoring the washing still to be pegged on the line.

35

"Oh, what a to–do! Do I look simply awful?" she chattered, dispelling the last remnants of panic.

"Very modern, Tabs. Very a–la–mode!"

We chuckled at this nonsense, she pretending to box my ears with her soft little hands. How they stayed so soft was a mystery to me for she was no stranger to hard work. Getting a kitchen chair, I sat behind her, putting a trousered knee either side of her shoulders, as I feathered and trimmed around the rescue site, she leaning into me as I rendered the chop–job less obvious.

"All done," I announced. She turned and batted her eyes up at me.

"Am I just beautiful? Shall I make it to the silver screen?" she joshed.

"Lovely, well, better than Bogart at any rate."

Tabitha howled with laughter and ran to the mirror inside, brushing past me through the doorway, as comfortable in my home as her own. I couldn't say the same back, but then, she had a fearsome housekeeper in the shape of old Mrs. Irvine to deter the most intrepid explorer.

Tabitha took no notice of the old battleaxe's dark looks and acerbic asides; she had known 'Mrs. Irv' forever, Mrs. Irv being hired by Tabitha's father to care for the house, Tabitha and her brothers in his many absences. He was something high up in the Ministry of Defence. Her elder brothers were already in the Navy and RAF when war broke out, so it was left to Tabitha and Mrs. Irv to maintain order at Greystones for the duration.

I picked my way through the muck, past my first marital home. No birds flew here; flies filling the void. I thought of my marriage and the rare confetti floating through crisp April air to the carolling of St. Elphin's bells.

I was an orphaned twenty–one when we wed, war broke out the year before, and Andrew was a Gunner in the RAF, not really expecting – or expected – to outlast the war. He was charming and dashing, full of fun and spirit, exciting to be around. Tabitha's eldest brother brought him home on leave several times in succession, bringing oranges and chocolates, rare treats igniting only cupboard love in my venal heart. Andrew lost his parents early in the war along with his home, so he came to Greystones instead; a lark ending in marriage, misery, parenthood and death.

Peering through empty window frames, I recognised previously cherished possessions only by approximate size and location. Some of the roses were still discernible on the wallpaper by the tiny fireplace. My mother's brass coal—scuttle lay greenly in the mud beside the cold, wet hearth.

Overlaying the room, the house, the whole lost village, was the memory—scape of what had been. Pale blue curtains fluttering in the breeze, the peppery scent of tall lupins carrying through the open window. William hiding under the counterpane on the bed, chuckling merrily at his game, awaiting delicious discovery. Much like now, I supposed.

The big old door of Greystones now stood open, tiny bare footprints dimpling the mud on the steps, leading me in. I followed them inside the great hall, starting slowly up the grand staircase, slipping at times, hoping against all reason that Tabitha would pad up behind me, make some terrible joke, keep me company, furnish me with answers. Instead, memories surged and coloured this mausoleum with life and light.

There, in the library to the right, I could see the slimy lump that had been the writing desk at which I sat, coldly composed with the help of Tabitha's father's brandy, writing Andrew that following his leave home I was now pregnant with our first child. Lies dripped from Tabitha's fountain pen, blotting the tissue thin paper, describing my happiness and contentment, informing him of the work done to fix the bomb damage at the dam, "...and again, my love, I'm so very glad it was another Gunner A. Delaney listed missing—presumed—KIA. Naturally, I hope he too is found safe and well soon. Communications leave as much to be desired as ever, but I hope you receive this letter, darling. I must confess on paper as I could not in person, for a while there I thought myself a widow!"

To the left, the great kitchen and its table, huge and solid still, where Tabitha skinned an unfortunate rabbit caught by the local poacher and left as 'tithe'. Mrs. Irv was out visiting a fellow battleaxe on her day off, so we were free to plot and plan as I nursed my darkling baby and schemed for our future. With ears snipped off, tiny blue bonnet on, and a pillowslip blanket securely wrapped around its naked pink carcass, my decoy was ready to present to the minister — a sweetly squeamish soul with smeared glasses and a habit of chewing pencils to splinters when deep in thought.

Tabitha had informed him — after the birth, after the discovery of my boy's beautiful brown skin and curly black hair, after hours of discussion, nursing, and tears, — that my child had been born too early, just a slip of a thing, and to please visit for comfort and discussion of funeral arrangements at 2pm sharp as I was distraught and would need bed soon after.

My plans to pass off this child as my husband's, my hopes that the dates were wrong and he *was* the father, were now for naught. My anonymous air−raid comforter had left me with more than a guilty memory.

We snuggled the sleeping William into an open drawer in the old servants' quarters under the eaves, with a hot water bottle for comfort and a sucker in his mouth. The minister kept his visit brief; I felt my soul squirm as I accepted his words of condolence and sympathy. He would spare me as much pain as he could, he said, and arrange the funeral for tomorrow at ten. He knew the perfect spot and would get Arnold, gravedigger and coffin− maker, to bring the receptacle round beforehand. He made a shushing noise and hushed away offers of payment from Tabitha.

The doctor was in the next big town dealing with air−raid casualties, he would certify the poor infant himself in the doctor's absence and allow us time to decently mourn and move on. Then, as he left, he reassured me that he was sure I would be a fine mother someday, God works in mysterious ways, my dear. He surely did.

Up, up the creaking, slippery stairs. Following the flashes of fur, I found our old bedroom, where I recovered from the birth and mock—death, where Tabitha fed me vegetable stew and horrible wholemeal toast. William was a good, quiet little boy. Tabitha took to playing the radio loud and long to cover any squawks or cries when Mrs. Irv was about. Those first few years of sneaking and laughing, hiding and loving, were golden; indeed, in my memory of it all, no matter the weather, all is cast in a glow.

It was difficult pretending grief every time Andrew came home on leave, but this became easier as my bond with William strengthened, and our separations grew harder. And I had to resist Andrew's advances. Nursing William meant leaking around Andrew, so clothing was essential, and I had to make excuses and keep darting off to Greystones on non—existent errands; even in the middle of the night I had to sneak from our marital bed and feed my young man.

The war took its toll on Andrew, the daredevil young man maturing into a bitter, brooding adult. Lacking the words to approach the subject, I could only glean scant ideas of his harrowing war work from newsreels at the pictures, and articles in the papers. I found him watching me with narrowed, speculative eyes that made me clumsy; all I could do to diffuse the tension was give him a kiss or a second drink. Then go to Greystones to fetch another bottle from their cellar.

I had planned a more systematic search from the cellar up, but glimpses of fur and wafts of sodden dog led me through certain rooms saturated with memories and stinking water until I came to Tabitha's old suite at the back of the house.

Entering, I felt like I'd walked in on an intimate conversation hastily hushed, but I could see no—one there. Everyone but me was watching the main event as I moved through the darkened house. Her suite had consisted of three adjoining rooms: sitting room, bedroom and bathroom. The old wood panelling, original to the house, had warped and cracked off the walls in some areas. Picture frames still sat on tables, now blackened and anonymous.

My chest tightened as I remembered the last time I was here. Muck had been involved then as now. Andrew was at the pub with friends, so I had seized the opportunity to clean out the henhouse with William. It was an exceptionally cold winter's day so we'd slid about, falling over in the filth several times; William chuckling till his breath came in hiccups, Jed barking in excitement, as much his second mother as Tabitha.

After, we went up to her rooms for a bath and hot cocoa. Tabitha sat on the floor drying William, ever the wriggler, while I sat on the edge of the sofa combing out her gloriously soft hair. The fire crackled and spat in the fireplace, the air smelling of soap and burning pine. My boy was serenading us with "Baa baa b'ack sheep", to the tune of something else. I reckoned I had about half an hour of bliss left before my return to the marital state. William stroked Jed's belly while Tabitha carefully rubbed his tight ebony curls. Then a low growl rose in Jed's throat, not directed at William but the door behind us.

"Go! Hide, my angel!"

William ran through to the bedroom with Jed as the living room door crashed open. Andrew staggered into the room, crying "The dam's bursting! We've got to go…" his voice died for a second as he took in our state of undress and flushed intimacy "you… you WHORE!"

"No, Andrew!" I protested, but in just a few steps he had grabbed a handful of my hair and swung a furious fist to my temple. It all went red and black and fuzzy.

I came to in the back of a truck, an ashen Andrew stroking my throbbing face with a tenderness I didn't know he had. His handsome face was scratched and bleeding, his arms red too, puncture marks and rips painfully visible. It took a while to come round fully, but when I did the sudden comprehension made me vomit bitter fluid over my husband. He barely flinched, but wiped my face and slowly, carefully, quietly said

"I couldn't find him. I'm so sorry, love, I tried, but that dog… I don't know what Tabitha will do when she finds out. I thought… I thought you and she were… all those visits and errands, the secrecy… you could have told me she'd had a kid. I'd have understood."

"We have to go back, where are we, we can still get him, Jed'll let me, quick, now —" my voice rising to alert the driver, but Andrew, tears leaking from his hollowed eyes, murmured

"It's too late. I'm so sorry, it's too late. Thorndale's totally underwater now. They reckon we'll be safe when we get to Penketh Lee. The shoddy repairs, this cold — the dam's cracked like an egg. I tried to get the boy, I really truly did." I believed him. I needed to. My boy. My beautiful boy. I howled with grief, with loss, with guilt, with shame. My little angel. My William.

"Where's Tabitha, why didn't she get him?" when at last I could speak again.

"She was in shock, she thought you were dead when I… well, she was carrying you outside for help, wouldn't let me touch you, till the lads in the truck told her about the dam going. She tried to get back in but she's not even dressed, she hadn't a chance in her smalls, I made her help get you on board and she told me about the boy, that he'd be hiding in her suite, but that dog…"

He shook his head. "She's in one of the other vehicles, helping that woman with the seven kids. She'll be thinking I got her son out safe. Oh Christ!" he buried his head in me, crying, "How could I leave the child to drown? How?" I died inside. My body has gone through the motions since, but my soul long since sank to purgatory, to the special section reserved for unfit mothers.

And now I've come back for my son, seven years too late. Andrew spoke with Tabitha the next day, breaking the news in private, dealing with her anguish with a stiff upper lip. His manner toward myself remained unchanged, so I could only assume she did not correct him when he informed her of the secret demise of her son.

I never saw Tabitha again, I couldn't bear to. My guilty grief was a raw unspoken barrier to friendship which might have mellowed given time. But not long after the flood I read she'd died in an accident. A real one, not like Andrew's. I can feel her warmth echoing in this dirty tomb across the years. Now I hear Jed whining next door. She's in pain but trying not to show it. And I think I can hear muffled sobs, a lonely noise in a desolate place.

I move past the rotten, sodden bed, past the dresser, and see movement in its oval mirror. There's Jed, in the corner, pink tongue panting, pulling herself along, painfully slowly, using just her front legs as her back is clearly broken. She gets to the wall and gnaws at the panelling till her teeth break, still she desperately carries on, white fragments on the wooden floor at her feet.

He's in the priest hole. We showed him it once, while playing hide and seek, training him in how to play so he would never be discovered by Mrs. Irv or his 'uncles'. The poor child was too small to reach the catch that let the panel swing open, not an issue when mummy or Tabitha are coming to find you. If you didn't know which knot to press on the outside, you'd never even know it was there. I could hear him wailing now.

"Mummy, Tabby, it's too dark in here! I want out! Mummy, out! Tabby, out now! P'ease? I say p'ease? P'ease!" Sobbing his little heart out. Oh God, I could imagine the water slowly seeping in, cold and dark and scary. Or did the air fail first? Did he fall asleep? Please, let him have just fallen asleep. I turned to the priest hole, sidestepping the pathetic mess of Jed's skeleton in the mud, and said to the terrified child of long ago, "Mummy's here, mummy's got you, mummy's here, mummy's got you," over and over.

My fingers clumsily pressed the warped wood, jiggling it till the catch gave and the door yawned open. He looked up at me, painfully hopeful, fingernails broken and red, overlaying the tiny bones and rags heaped in the small dark hole. I held out my hand and felt the skin crackle and pinch with the piercing cold it encountered there. I think I felt the weight of him as he clung to me in enormous relief, not abandoned, not alone, not forgotten, but loved, cherished, adored, remembered.

"My darling boy, my darling angel, mummy's here, everything's alright. I've got you." I lullabied, reassuring us both. Outside, the sky had darkened and I heard the grumble of thunder.

I closed my eyes in his crinkly wet hair, smelling the soap of his bath more than the odour of wet dog or the stench of wet death and mud nearby. He was so cold. I felt his chest stop heaving, felt the tiny flannelette pyjamas, his small bottom, his head nuzzled shyly into my neck for comfort. Then I felt Jed lean against my legs, the thump thump of her wagging tail.

"My good boy. You're my good boy," I murmured.

Outside the storm burst and raged. Wind gusted round us, battering us with rain through the window frame. I could barely feel it. Hours passed in minutes. I stood comforting my son – "I'm here, my darling. I'm here." – as the water began to lap around my ankles.

Yellow

"I'm learning Japanese."

Gran threw my bacon straight from the griddle into the sink. It sizzled and spat in the drips pooling under the taps.

Three words she'd heard as 'I hate you' or 'I'd kill him again if I could'. Three words it took weeks to say.

"Why would you do a thing like that?"

She waited, lips pursed and arms folded tight across her chest. I guessed she was tucking her hands away before they hit me. She knew I'd walk out over that; she needed to vent a little first.

"I like the language; the culture is… interesting. The food's delicious. And it's great for my CV—"

She turned her head and spat in the sink.

My grandfather fought for freedom. Freedom to live, love, and worship as you see fit. The way grandma tells it, he went over there to kill the Yellow Peril. She didn't think then they had the cunning to kill him instead.

And I don't know that they did. I don't know. I know he was shot down and captured, kept squatting in a bamboo cage for days at a time. And came home whole but in pieces, the same to look at but not to talk with, never again. I know there was never rice in the house, or at neighbourhood weddings, not in our bags, anyway. We threw crumbs or confetti. If someone forgot, grandfather turned white and walked off at a brisk march. I know he died slowly of a cancerous spleen, my grandma at his side.

Did they kill him? That I don't know. But my family, my grandma, hold that the torture brought the cancer to his spleen. They think Asia killed him.

"Your grandfather..."

She was shaking, her eyes moist, face crimson.

"He was very brave. It's awful what happened. I don't mean to upset you..."

"But you're doing it anyway? Huh!" She turned her back, muttering "Go."

I stood, crossed the kitchen to the door. Said "I love you."

Again with the spitting in the sink. She was muttering something in acid whispers as I left, fingers rubbing the silver locket lying heavy on her chest, eyes pinched shut as I followed the path past the kitchen window.

I walked to the church, met my brother inside.

"Did you tell her?"

"I tried."

He clasped my hand, looking me in the eye.

"Perhaps you could try again?"

I shook my head, no.

Golden daffodils and the palest cream hyacinths standing succulent by the altar, I wondered what I should choose for the big day. His family would appreciate chrysanthemums and there would be no−one there to mind, now.

The Rescue

Ria could feel it cooling at her breast as she scurried with the others through the dark, down to the desperate shore. Her clogs skidded slightly on storm spattered rocks, life on the island schooling her in predicting the locations of larger patches of seaweed. White rimmed clouds, the storm silhouetted by a waxing moon, lent ease to her embarrassment. She was but one figure among many.

The menfolk were mainly spread along the fingers of raggedy rock that dug into the North Sea, their figures bent either into the wind or into the froth, rescuing casks, timber and oddments before the precious shipment was swept out to the hungry deeps. Without so much as a glance cast behind, her Douglas marched stiffly to join them, his blond hair catching the eye of the minister praying with hands protected in deep pockets, the wind not daring to tumble his hat away.

"Douglas! Ready yourself, there's a few still afloat. Go give Stevie a help," he shouted, pointing a pale hand to the left before masking the tremble again with his pocket.

Seeing her stumbling gait and clumsy waddle, rags stuffed thick between her legs to stem the flow, still her secret, hers and Dougie's, he called to her:

"Ria, you shouldn't be out in this, hen."

Acid burnt the depths of her throat, she could smell vomit approaching the back of her nose, and sniffed back the rising panic. If he should see…

"No sir, I'm fine, I'm needed here. Please…"

There was a shout through the crash and fizz of waves dashing the shore. A tiny vessel, vulnerable and dainty on the swells surging past the wreck, was approaching the coastline, its oars splashing white in the moonlight. A gang of islanders ran to meet it, the minister joining them, praying for lost and losing souls.

Ria shuffled along the shoreline, allowing the fierce wind to guide her way, salt spray stinging her eyes and the abrasions on her face. Her breasts itched with milk, uncomfortably hot despite the chill night air. But she would not weep. It was not their way.

Handsome and hardy, Dougie rolled a large barrel with Stevie above the high tide mark, wedging it in place with the others using a lump of the grey granite that littered the area. Stevie's head bobbed with chatter, and the friends stood for a moment, slapping hands in happiness. Salt pork, she guessed, maybe water biscuits. Not rum or small beer anyway. The minister was right, the Lord shall provide unto the faithful few. Not that Ria had ever doubted this fact, but she knew her Dougie had been worried about the harsh winter ahead. Now the island's resources were more suitable, she was sure things would be better between them. And since it was just them … well, it would get back to normal, wouldn't it?

She'd spoken with her mother once, about the mysteries of married life, and her mother had said with eyes that slid like melted butter to the chair, to the floor, that the meek would inherit the earth. Ria had been confused at the time. Tonight she better understood, though she couldn't agree. There was an ocean of difference between being quiet and cowed, a difference that her mother didn't seem equipped to fathom. Nor her sister who was 'in bed with a cold' as often as not. Ria had endured many a sniffle, but never one that involved a scald, or sneezing till your eyes purpled and your nose bled. But she never questioned, she never pried, for that was not the island way. In a community as remote as theirs, where little was for the individual, and most for the common or greater good, the illusion of privacy was valued as highly as that of their unswerving faith.

Grateful for the sea's bounty, she allowed her mind to slip away from the vessel nearing the hostile shore, and the thick rope the hopeful were casting through salt water, desperate for it to reach strong sand–speckled hands. Her swollen feet followed their usual path through a fault–line in the rocks, broken lumps acting as irregular stairs when she passed along them daily with the low tide, seeking driftwood, ropes, and the big skittering crabs sometimes stranded in the rock pools. Steamed on the fire then served with butter, they were her Dougie's favourite food. And she liked to make him happy. Wives do.

It was a quirk in the geography of the place that meant this little cove collected some of the better logs and trees washed from foreign shores and vessels to their barren island. The wind made some funny noises here, howling like abandoned children as it rushed through the gaps in the rocks. Some of the gatherers were more superstitious than the minister cared to admit, gossiping as they mended nets about kelpies and their kind. Ria had her faith in the Lord, and trusted that He would look after her, there at least.

Barnacles clustered rough under her hands but the cold damp air numbed her skin so she was barely aware of them. The cooling bundle was harder to ignore. Her sweet Scottish voice joined that of the storm, crooning a lullaby, comforting only herself in the lonely ink–blue bay. Bladderwrack popped under her feet, the seaweed less of a hazard here as she had damp walls of rock to steady her on her way and shield her from the worst of the wind. Soon her clogs crunched on the pockets of sand and shingle to be found there, where she had written her name with twigs as a child. Pausing for breath, exhausted by the day's events, Ria heard the clattering of tackety boots hastening after her on the rocks. His pale hair glowed as if lit from within, but shadows hid his features as the bruising hid her own. Despite the discomfort, her cheeks twitched a nervous smile of appeasement, a grimace in the gloom.

"What're you doing here? There's plenty to be done on the shore, I'll not have them saying I married an idle wretch."

His hand was rough on her shoulder, his tone as rough on her ears.

"Dougie, my love, this cove collects uncommon wreckage, and the minister was pleased for—" but here his other hand flashed quick in the black, loosening her teeth, quieting her from answering back. Lip bleeding against rough edges, her tongue quivered against the tiny wound, worrying at it as a bitch licks her new—whelped pups. Her eyes blinked against the salt, and the injustice.

Now he sneered in an ugly voice so unlike their wedding vows:

"An expert on the sea, are you? I'll see you swim, if there's nothing there," and he hauled her in a halting fashion toward the waves dashing the shore. "I'll *not* have you embarrassing me."

She stumbled, unable to catch herself properly as his fingers made tight purchase on her shawl. But on they went, the master and his wretch, till the breakers blew brine in their faces. The wind whipped her heavy skirts between her legs, further hindering their progress as the storm clouds sped from the moon. The delay seemed to please him, the moonlight glistening on his bared teeth, spittle frothing from the corners of his grinning mouth. So cruel, she thought, so vicious, yet this is the mouth of the man I married, the mouth I kissed, the mouth that told me he loved me.

His boot slithered on the kelp lying in splayed fingers like a mermaid's forgotten glove on the rocks at the edge. Breaking his gaze from her terrified face, his too—wide eyes saw a large basket in the rock pool to their right. The wicker was crushed on one side, the splintered weave snagging on the rocks, assisting in wedging it there till a higher tide. A last wrench of rough cloth, grinding her arm bone beneath, then release.

She stumbled, the wind catching her, righting her balance before she tumbled to the crashing depths, the shore dropping off steeply beside them. But he had loosened the shawl, and in one heavy gust, the billowing fabric soared free, releasing their delicate daughter to the deep. The hurt was bundled up inside her from before, swaddled from the afternoon's events. Pale froth floated fragile on the wind, free from its mother the sea. Ria yearned to join it, to follow the tiny white bundle being dashed against the rocks to her left. Strands of hair whipped against her wounded face, punishing her for letting go, though she hadn't, really she hadn't; again he had forced a separation. Again she was made to let go.

Turning for a last look at the father of her child as he pawed at the wreckage, she felt him clawing her in the kitchen, hauling the baby out. Then the horrible heavy wet thud, forever in her ears, of her husband dashing it to the stone—flagged floor when he saw the absence between its legs. She released the rage. A clog came away from her leaden foot as she clambered down, no longer top heavy with the hours dead infant.

Dougie didn't notice her in her fury. He raised a rock above his flaxen head, the disappointment on his face writ large about the contents of the crib below. He was as practical about his intended actions as if the child were merely a triplet lamb, a drain on the flock. Now she could hear the squalling, real against the deception of the rock—narrowed wind. One solid push and he had stumbled over. Over and down. His hair soon vanished beneath the waves.

Bending over the basket, Ria gently fingered the oilcloth protecting the baby. It was very small, face still squashed and red from the journey to meet its mother. She undid the rough twine lashing it to its vessel, and examined its hopeful face in the pale light of the moon. Scenting milk nearby, her breasts answering the child's call for food with creamy drips, it wriggled in her arms, turning its face expectantly toward her chest.

She quickly scanned her surroundings for witnesses. Alone but for the baby, she tossed the damaged crib after her husband before replacing her clog, hurrying for the shelter of the stairs. She sat down, the wind moaning through the rocks around her, and loosened her top, milk spraying the baby's face with pale freckles before it latched on. She felt the release, her breast soon cool, and snaked her little finger into the corner of the nursling's mouth, swapping sides with ease.

The storm was passing now, the night clear and cold, the sky spattered with stars. Nooked in on the steps, she unwrapped the child with her free hand, enough to see its navel and gender. The dark, crusty little stump told Ria all she needed to know. What lay beneath told her she held all the island desired.

Once the baby had slowed in his suckling, she felt him grow warm, limp and contented in her arms as he drifted to sleep, eventually loosing his mouth from her teat. Covering herself again, she rocked him in her arms, her own salt water spilling down her cheeks; for her murdered daughter, her marriage, and her decision. Stumbling, she carried her precious bundle up the stairs, along the coastal path to the rest of the island, finding them throwing back the ropes of the survivors. The minister was lending their hands strength through prayer, as the faces in the vessels realised the islanders' intent in letting them perish.

As the families were washed to deeper waters, her son nuzzled into her neck, eyes closed tight against the world.

The Creature in the Coal

Heat wavered the air as they sped along the tracks, Cal in nought but a pair of short trousers held up with rope as he fuelled the beast. He'd swayed into a rhythm soon enough that morning, shovelling the dusty black lumps from left to right, left to right, bunker to furnace, warm to hot, warm to hot until he was dancing in the heat. The driver peeeep'd the whistle atop the old engine, and Cal slowed his swivelling, waiting for the pat on his shoulders that signalled a stop. It came, the hand callused and old. Cal moved up the coal pile, agile and experienced enough to know where to step and where would lead to a sliding fall. As they coasted into the station where ladies with umbrellas and damp skirts and servants awaited their train, the driver handed a jug of water back to the boy.

Warm as blood, black motes skimming the surface, it tasted fantastic. Cal drank the lot, great draughts in noisy gulps finished with a final burp of satisfaction. The driver was on the step by the platform, talking to the stationmaster, so Cal knew he had a few minutes rest yet. Perhaps there was a deal of luggage out there, he thought, or perhaps somebody fainted. He minded his mama fainting, when she got the letter during the war. *Flump*, straight to the fresh washed floor of their apartment. The postman had helped move her to the kitchen, poured her some gin. He wondered where she'd got to now.

A body that's tired enough will find comfort anywhere it falls upon. Cal was tired, but not so tired as to find the hillock of crumbled carbon anywhere near comfortable. He fidgeted a little, then realised it was a ragged rock in his back that was the problem. The size of a football, the same near oval shape, he held it in his lap and marvelled at its shine. He could almost see the white of his teeth in it, but the surface was rippled as if a sea of tar and oil had set in an instant of ebony storm. Turning it this way and that on his knee, he realised it wasn't just the usual jagged black to be shovelled unnoticed into the flames: it was something different, and new.

He spat on it, wiped what little coal dust there was away with his thumb and the leg of his shorts. Turned it in the warm orange glow of the flickering flames.

Some kind of animal, something... unseen. Not like the zoo or the pictures he saw sometimes when he went into the library for a heat in the winter. This was very *very* different.

He shook it, finding the heft of it pleasant in his grasp. Held it closer to the furnace maw, wondered if his eyes were playing tricks on him. Counted the eyes and prominent teeth, the knobbles of feet and paws. Stroked the line of its neck and back, and the thick tail it wrapped round itself, like a stray riding out a storm.

He'd never found anything more than the odd shell or leafprint in the coal before. Well, once he *had* found that dead lady's purse, but the driver gave him a dollar for it and he let it go. He'd never found himself a pet before. His hands seemed to stroke it through the coal, knowing where it liked the pressure best, and where not to venture for fear of waking it from its doze.

He realised the driver had been calling him, perhaps a few times now, and without thinking he jumped down. Usually he'd check who was out there first, wipe his face on the inside of his shirt, get cleaned up, put it on then go.

"Oh! What is *that*, that creature there!"

She had soft hands but a stricken sharp voice, and her maid took her arm, supporting her and fending off a faint.

"Miss, it's my pet, miss…" Cal said before he realised.

She meant him.

Imago

Flakes like confetti or what she remembered of wild cherry blossom, littered the armchair in which she sat and waited. For Him. She tried not to scratch, not to shed any more of herself onto the dingy green arms that held her as she listened to the radio crackle and whine.

Then He was there. Scraping, nuzzling, rasping His stubble against her poor sore elbows, licking up her litter with a yellow—grey tongue. He'd told her He had a cure, and she'd been desperate and believed.

Her condition had only worsened since He'd left her in the cellar. No creams, no ointments, and a steady diet of all the things that made it worse. Tomatoes. Cloves. Honey. She knew what she could and couldn't do, and so did He after the Consultation that led her here. Now instead of patches of extra cells, thickening sore and silver, rosetted with livid pink against her normal skin, she looked like one of the dried husks of fish she used to stare at in the Asian supermarket by the Temples. Even her hair had gone.

Lately He'd been overfeeding her, refusing to leave her in peace, to stop eating her decay and sickening her as she withdrew behind misting eyes, until she finished her plateful and curled up in the odious chair, the one piece of furniture in the place.

She might have been naked, but the pale flakes diminished her nudity. And they were all He had eyes for when He entered the sweaty fetid cloud of a room like a gull taunting a thunderstorm, so she didn't care, not really. Fed, full, she just wanted to sleep. No, *needed* to. Curling up, knees tight to her chest, she mumbled something and from the door He watched, and smiled.

It took a few weeks, but then she was ready. As was He.

This was the best bit, the part of the process that made all the risk worthwhile. That made Him worthy. That guaranteed Him a place at the Gates.

The cracking thrilled him, it always did and he had to restrain himself from helping Her. Soon She was open, but still damp and confused. Opening the door wide, front door already gaping and swaying slightly in the cool night breeze, he crooned to her with need.

Out She flew, and She was *beautiful*. Palest blue and cocoa brown wings, multifaceted eyes in peacock petrol hues, and a dusky pink body the like of which he'd never seen, not in any of his girls to date.

Job done, Beauty nurtured and released, he fell upon the empty cocoon, feasting on all that She chose to leave behind.

Luck is in the Leftovers

She *had* told him not to do it, not to swing it round the apartment as a shimmering sword, not to whirl and swirl through the thousand breaths of age that lingered in the silent room. And now, inevitably, he had knocked something down, something that watched him reproachfully from the tatami through splinters of twinkling glass. The frame was intact, the photo barely scratched but exposed now, naked, to the museum of sighs.

Kaito as a baby, his grandparents sitting beside, uncomfortable but happy in their new roles, stepping back another generation onto unfamiliar ground. He knew they loved him and wished him well, but they were not not NOT his parents. And although family, they were relations layered with regret.

Grandfather would be angry. His voice would not rise, nor his hand, but the look of reproach would grey the room, and guilt would sour Kaito's supper tonight. So he made his escape.

They had asked him, many times, to let it down, pack it away, keep it aside for other times, other places. But since he was six, he could not. He slept with it, his arms sticky and red where they met harsh plastic, and carried it with him wherever he went; beach, shops, the factory, school.

Comfort was light in his hands, an inflatable golf club his mother bought from a vending machine in his last weekend with her, her breath captured with his father's in the plastic toy they had struggled to fill, laughter bubbling within.

Seeking a substitute for his mother's caress that did not exist, not on this plane, Kaito's feet carried him to the beach to look for his girl. Down he went, over white cobbles framed with a green grout of weeds, past the spattered grey tideline of shells and small bones to the golden sand by the sea, but as with the days before she was nowhere to be seen. His regret ebbed and flowed with the lapping waves.

To be sure, he walked along the damp flat edging the water, past the braille of shiny black pebbles speckling perfect beige. Left, along to the pale cliff perched on a darker, crumbling base, the sea seeping insidious through the gap, small circles of smooth appearing for moments amongst the froth as dark clouds sought to shed their heavy load.

It had rained the night his parents died, cars sliding and spinning, his grandparents coming to the hospital, holding him all the way home. He had wailed, cried, and mourned their passing, feeling bad about being left behind. It was his piano recital they had been going to.

But Grandmother had held his chin between finger and thumb, waited till he saw her truth in those old brown eyes, and said:

"Luck exists in the leftovers."

Kaito was not entirely sure what the proverb suggested, but he knew she meant it kindly, and was content, for a while.

Back along the beach, he thought he saw movement amongst the waves. Why did she not come closer? She must know it was him, even with his stubborn hair brushed and smoothed down with water. He missed her. A cookie might do it, he'd snatched one from the kitchen as he left. Kaito didn't know if turtles liked cookies, but they were one of his favourites, so maybe she would. He could see it floating gold on the gun—grey waves then slowly sinking out of sight. Would it bring her over? Then he saw what he'd taken for Yuzuki was just a knot of driftwood, and the loneliness ached once more.

Teenagers had left a bonfire to smoulder from the night before, a relic of good times past. Salt smells vied with the acrid smoke for a taste of his nose, but he was snuffling with sadness and noticed neither one. The boy sat, knees to his chest, still cuddling the sweaty stem of the golf club, cold moisture from the sand seeping through the seat of his shorts as he listened to the *ssshhh* of the surf, remembering a time last year when the light was the same.

It had been nearly dusk, details fading with the dark as with the passage of time, and he'd been looking for the glint of pirate's treasure in the sand when he heard a strange snapping noise from the inlet up the beach. There was a small horseshoe of cliff there, a puckering of the coastline in a pout or a kiss. Kaito had been told to stay away from the area when the tide was rising or risk being trapped and drowning as he was swept against the cold white rock. He had, very carefully, wandered closer, the rabid froth of an incoming tide delineating the danger clearly against the darkening sand, the noise of snapping growing louder and now joined by a tantalisingly gritty sound, as if small boats were being scraped ashore.

Kaito was nearly upon them when the wind blew along a lingering cloud, letting the rising moon's light bleach the bay. Two huge turtles were fighting, one snapping at the other, clumsily aggressive in the sand. He watched with curiosity and awe and no thought of intervening till the turtle suffering a tail— nip turned its head and seemed to meet his tired eyes. Moonlight glinted liquid diamonds on her face, and he realised she was crying. Kaito neither knew nor cared that these amazing beasts do so simply to shed salt from their systems once on dry land. He only knew that an animal was in trouble and for once he, Kaito, could do something to help it. Arms whirling, hands clapping, feet kicking fireworks of sand, the turtles soon parted and left him with only their tracks on the shore.

59

His grandparents understood the boy's need for solitude and reconciliation with the sweeping forces of nature. They hoped the calming beauty of the Pacific would soothe their little orphan's soul. Many evenings later, his grandfather took him with a flask of hot tea to the shore to show him something special. With the moonlight spilling like coconut milk on washed smooth sand they sat, the boy leaning into the man for warmth, and waited for a wonder, tea scalding their tongues in the salt night air. Kaito noticed there were many birds ghosting along the beach too. Then it happened and the gulls clustered and dipped and tore.

"What is it, Grandfather?"

The old man sipped the last of the tea.

"The miracle of life;" he shook drips from the cup "and the necessary acceptance of death."

They stood, dusting the sand off their trousers, then made their way closer to the screeching scratching seagulls. Kaito saw the birds were feasting on little dark things that seemed to be magically sprouting from the sand. It wasn't oil; these oblongs were moving about on their own. Squatting by the torrent, he picked one up.

It was a tiny turtle, soft and cute, slapping his hand with small flippers as it tried to get away. Returning the creature to the sand, Kaito was horrified when a gull grabbed it and made it its own. The old man watched with interest as Kaito shooed away the hungry birds which just kept landing in another place, at another turtle, flapping about as he tried to save even one small life.

Soon the sand lay still once again, the gulls grew quiet, and the survivors began another battle beneath the waves. Two figures stood, tall and small, and left for home, death done with for another day.

Kaito tried not to think about why Grandfather had stood by in silence. Perhaps, he reasoned, to accept two large deaths means accepting them all. To fight one is to lose sight of your place in nature. He slept uneasily that night.

The next day, he walked with his grandmother to the beach. The chill raised goose bumps on his legs, the white on the waves matched his chattering teeth, and the pines shifted from side to side on the cliff tops as strangers do at bus—stops trying to keep warm. But Kaito remembered the night before and asked his grandmother for a swim.

"I want to see… just see if any made it."

"It is too cold, my dear. I can tell you that some will have made it, they always do, but they will be far away now, out to sea, dodging the dolphins and fish until they have grown too big and hard for others to eat them easily."

The boy still looked forlorn, and so like his father. She sighed.

Still, his eyes flicked with worry to the grey and white enormity before them.

"Remember, little one, luck exists in the leftovers."

Her arm around his small shoulders, so like her son's at that age, they began the journey home.

After that, he'd visited daily. When the water warmed he managed an occasional swim in the glittering ocean, hoping to see the small dark oval of a survivor or the gold bullion of a pirate's treasure amongst the worms of blue rope and discarded cans that lay on the seabed. One day he swam for a barrel he saw near the surging wake of a fishing boat, and was surprised when it dived below, but even more surprised when he looked back and realised how far he'd come from shore. Paddling, panicked, he felt the current tug tiring legs, salt leaking down his face to mingle with the sea. Then the 'barrel' resurfaced, took a long slow measure of the boy, and distracted him enough to let him breathe.

This was Yuzuki, a loggerhead turtle, marked fawn and white as a flattened giraffe from above and the colour of creamy butter from below. The plates on her back rose and fell in a range of tiny mountains, as beautiful in symmetry as Fujiyama. She swam round Kaito in a wide lazy loop, and watched with her head bobbing above the water until he strode from the shallows with relief. From then, Kaito found if he stood on the beach and watched she would come. Not all the way out. Sometimes to the shallows, sometimes just off shore, but he could tell it was her, he saw the way she splashed a salt froth with her flippers before heading back to the depths. If the sun was right she raised rainbows. Kaito called her Yuzuki after his mother's childhood cat, hoping to tempt her back for a look.

Sitting on the beach now, uncalled, the bonfire crackling as embers greyed to ash, he felt cold and abandoned, smaller than before. When would his grandparents come? It wasn't them he wanted, not really, just his mum and dad, with their cuddles and tickles and funny pet names. Tears sidled down his cheeks to join the saltwater in the sand. They would come. They had to.

Kaito thought a little, about guilt and loss, fear and redemption. He stood up and started to strip, wobbling a little, until he had only his shorts and the golf club to protect him in the angry looking sea. Misogi is a cold, wet ritual with the hope of making good the only warmth throughout. Practised by ascetics and the guilt–ridden through many generations, there are usually prayers and salt to aid the quest for purity, and cold water to cleanse the shivering soul. Those who submit their bodies to the water are usually adult, but Kaito had grown–up feelings needing grown–up solutions.

Handle in hand, he sprinted for the ocean. Skinny legs pumping, he splashed through the hissing water, calling sorrow to the clouds as he dived in. The current accepted him, pulled him swiftly further and further out. Though good at swimming and adept at holding his breath, Kaito started to feel the first jitters of panic fluttering in his chest, moths of emotion struggling free from cocoons of common sense. It was a struggle, but he managed to get his head above water. Striding with shivering feet, he looked to the shore he'd left so carelessly behind. Turning to see if there were any boats he could signal to nearby, Kaito's breath burnt fire in his throat as he inhaled sea spray with fright.

Clutching the golf club as if it were his grandmother's neck at bedtime, he felt its hard nub of valve poke his face. He thought of the divers on the news last night, sampling seaweeds, avoiding ulcerous anemones and toothsome eels, trusting a tube to satisfy their lungs. Cold fingers popped the cap and he was about to bite down on the pipe to open it, hoping the air would last him to shore, when something tugged his shorts. Not a shark?!

Large, solid and slippery, it bumped his stomach. Kaito found himself looking into the old brown eyes of Yuzuki. She nudged his arms with a flipper. Biting the valve hard, feeling a wobbly tooth shift with the pressure, he kept one arm round the golf club and hooked the other round her neck. Hard, tight. She stretched nearly the length of him, his legs trailing behind.

Kaito heard a rush inside his head, memories swirling with the currents through his hair. He was growing dizzy, concentrating on holding on to life, Yuzuki, and the deflating golf club while his ears popped and sang and all manner of sticks and debris scratched past him. He wondered when, if, he should accept the will of the water and just let go. But the thought of his grandparents, who had already lost so much, searching at the water's edge helped him crook his arms round his saviours that little bit tighter.

Now it felt as though they were swimming up again. The water seemed clearer, though still dark. Soon their heads broke free of the sea. Kaito spat plastic from his aching jaws, gulped the air around them, licked stinging lips. Yuzuki towed him carefully along though she too had tired from their journey. His eyes adjusting, Kaito began to see shapes in the darkness, lit by a pale green light. Not a lantern or a lamp, but seemingly the rocks themselves. It could still only be afternoon, though time had paused as if to watch. They must be in a cave. Yuzuki brought him to a ledge and he staggered onto it, the rough granulations peculiar to his soaked soft feet, before flopping onto the cave floor a step above.

"Thank you, Yuzuki..." but she was gone.

The last of his strength went with her. His eyelashes knit together as if praying hands, and he was asleep.

63

Sitting up, Kaito realised his shorts were dry. It was quite warm here, despite the sea's constant cold presence, lapping the rocks to his side. Perhaps there were hot springs nearby, sending him warmth through the stone. His grandmother used them when her arthritis was bad, always inviting him to join her for a spell, but they reminded him of her sputtering rice cooker and he declined.

Standing, he stretched, yawning the ache from his jaws. Now would be a good time to find a way out.

There were a few hope filled fissures, deep and winding, that he'd followed to rock falls and dead−ends. At one of them he felt his mother's breath on his face, air whispering through gaps in the rubble, keeping the tomb alive. For now. He screamed for help until his throat hurt and tears threatened, a chorus of cries his only company in the void. Moving back towards the water, he realised the light was quite soothing, the same shade as her best jade earrings.

A splash at the water's edge: Yuzuki had returned, a fish trailing from her beak. She bobbed at the water's edge and Kaito realised she had brought him something to eat. Small and striped, its pink flesh was ready for him where Yuzuki had snapped it nearly in two. He thought of his grandmother's sashimi and ate, thanking Yuzuki for her kindness with every mouthful. Too soon, she sank away, leaving him with his memories and a comfortable belly.

His foot had found a dip of water by a rock−fall earlier, feeling thirsty, he went for another look. Water trickled past the stone, drips coming together in a hollow at the base. Kneeling in the dust, he cupped his hands and drank.

Perhaps two full days passed with sleep and hunger, thirst and urination, acting as his clocks. The warmth made him sleepy and after the first few naps he barely noticed the odd mineral smell of the rocks serving as his bed. His basic needs were taken care of; he was warm, fed and watered, and grateful for it. Yuzuki brought him fish and seaweed every couple of hours, splashing her fin in a froth to draw the boy near. After, he would stand at different rock—falls and shout till his voice coarsened; drink, and shout some more.

He could live there forever, really, he thought to himself. It was very peaceful, and warm, and the cavern had a strange beauty to it that would never change. Here, he was away from everyone, not just his parents. Whatever the weather, whatever the hour, whatever little details he had worried about up—side, things were constant here. No seasons. No storms. No birthdays, no funerals. A different world, indeed.

But increasingly, the drips of water filling his drinking pool made him wonder about his grandparents' weeping for him. He could picture his grandmother at lunch, arranging their bento boxes with delicious colours, before remembering, sighing, and taking it for the widow next door. She always gave him an extra pickle slice, the swirling pink and white inviting careful nibbles, first one stripe, then the other, as the miso cooled beneath fragrant steam. Grandfather folding him boats from his newspaper, noble junks for bath time, some of them unread. Sending him to the shop for matches, the change his to spend as he wished, tens of minutes passing as he eyed comics, sweets and toys, before choosing none, the coins more satisfying in his room. Sadness entered the void. No—one was aware of his life here; he must take charge of his own return. Now he longed to feel the warmth of the sun on his cheeks, see the soft pink tears of falling blossom, smell his grandfather's tobacco, and escape the numb refuge of this netherworld.

When Yuzuki rose through the water, he was waiting.

Slipping off the ledge, he chewed a mouthful of the greens she brought him for breakfast before slipping his arms round her firm, freckled neck. Deep breaths later, he gasped and they dived. It felt quicker than the first, but now the cold of the water shocked him to the bone. With tiny mountains digging into his chest, he watched the water lighten through stinging eyes, waiting for the warmth of the rising sun.

Miss

Every day the front door closes, and every day I wish I'd said goodbye.

I talk to my plants, telling them how she was always the prettiest girl, the one the boys caught and kissed, the one meant to leave this dead end town and Do Something.

But she never did.

I sit and count the commercials on TV from my chair by the veiled window. Three dead flies lie on the windowsill, legs clutched to shiny black chests as if in prayer. I'll have to speak to her about that. No–one will visit if they look in the window and spy *that*.

Perhaps the mailman will call. The TV announcer changes shift, marking time for my mid–morning coffee, and I guess we're not getting any mail today, so the mailman won't call. He'll be on Peach Avenue by now, blocks past our house, into the streets named after fruit trees and out of the avenues of Founding Fathers. We're on Adams Avenue, and not for the first time I think how much our street sounds like the punch line to the kind of bawdy joke Len's friends used to tell before they caught me looking.

The phone rings and I mute the TV, answer, voice bright: "Good morning?"

But she isn't checking on me. She never does.

It's a survey, and I want to talk to her, she sounds a nice young thing, but she asks me how many toilet rolls we use in a week and I hang up. Nice girls don't talk about *that*.

Nine more commercial breaks then it's time for lunch. My stomach isn't grumbling, but this is when Len and I used to stop whatever we were doing and enjoy lunch — and each other if we had the house to ourselves. I miss that. Not just the company, but everything.

The fridge beeps at me as I take too long taking the bowl out. Everything takes too long, now. Into the microwave, and I can already smell that she's skimped on the spices. Second day soup can be unforgiving to its creator; I root through the cupboard for seasoning as the machine *burrs* and my knees ache from standing. I used to walk miles.

She must have used up the last of the 'Happy Hoi Sin' mix, I can only find a new tin, unopened, with a stupid red circle on the front shouting 'New Recipe!!!' at me as if one exclamation mark wasn't enough.

I need to sit down. I wonder what she's having for lunch, and who with.

Her father bought me this table. It was when we were courting; I opened the front door one spring morning and there he was, sitting there with the smile he passed to his daughter — not that I ever see it now — and breakfast laid out for me under the old cherry tree. Pancakes, maple syrup, and the sweetest orange juice I'd ever tasted. We sat there in the shade as blossom fell softly in the breeze, floating in my juice till he fished the petals out. I wanted to lick his fingers and I knew then that he was the one for me.

She doesn't know it, but when she's away I move his portrait to the table. It's good to have eyes to gaze into as you eat. She told me I didn't need to check her dusting, that she does it right, she *always* does it right, and I know she does. I can see. But somehow, it doesn't come out that way.

She shouldn't have to work. There should be grandkids and a son—in—law for me to tease. She comes home so stressed, I can see it when she chews her lip, she's just like her father. I hoped maybe by me buying insurance, upping her figures, she'd get a raise or something. Maybe a nicer desk. Near a window. But no.

Ding! The light in the microwave goes out. Soup's ready. It takes a while to get it to the table, and I try to keep my hands steady, but I still spill some, and I click my tongue at this, curse my ailing body under my breath, then feel guilty. I'll no doubt spill more, my hand shakes when I eat, but I wipe it off our table anyway. She stained the dishcloth this morning, so I use that. I might as well.

I open the lid of the seasoning mix and sniff the brown powder within. It smells the same, I don't see what's so *new* about it, what warrants the fuss of three exclamation marks when one would do. I shake some over the soup in front of me, stir slowly as I read the ingredients. Then pause as I read four fatal letters, nestled in amongst the new recipe's pepper, cloves, and MSG.

Fish.

I'm allergic to fish. Not in that namby pamby way where celebrities bloat and children grow red—speckle rashes. Properly live—or—die allergic.

And she knows it. She just doesn't care enough to check.

I look at my husband. Leave the spoon in the bowl, go and turn off the TV.

That's better. I'll hear him now.

I wait a while, a long long while. It's cool enough to eat, if I choose.

And I do. Before I can't.

I think of how he messed as he lay dying in my arms, of the aromas and the embarrassment. Portrait in one hand, 'Happy Hoi Sin' mixture in the other, I make it to the bathroom down the hall. Lock the door, because I always do. It feels wrong not to, even when I'm just doing my teeth. Hold the rim of the bathtub and lower myself carefully as I grow dizzy and sway, sinking onto the fluffy cream bathmat with relief. Lie down and hold him on the floor.

My lips are tingling as from our first kiss.

I hold on till I hear her calling "Ma?"

Then again, almost tenderly,

"Ma?"

Slut's Pennies

Hands soft as his voice push and pull the pale dough, the air sweet and starchy in a cloud around him.

"Knead until your nails come clean," I tell him, the tin floured, ready and waiting. I watch him as I stir luncheon's rabbit stew, my other hand carefully still at my side. Slowly the spoon swirls through lumpy potato and circles of carrot, pink chunks pretty and growing tender in the fragrant stock. "I'll need your help shifting this off the stove, in a little while."

He winks, face reddening with the heat of the kitchen and, I flatter myself, his nearness to me. The chain of his fob watch sways with his vigour, and I notice he has removed the ring from his left hand prior to starting work, just as he does when he's seeing to me.

A grin dimples his cheeks as if he is four not forty and he shapes the dough into a coarse sausage before slapping it into the tin, then moves to the sink with his fingers by his face. He splashes his hands under the tap quickly, flicking me with droplets before drying them vigorously in the skirts around my rump, hands rubbing and kneading me, whiskers scouring my face in a kiss until her bell rings upstairs and he pulls back and shrugs.

"Duty calls."

"Will you be back for the stew?"

He's already slipped the ring on his finger, and nods as he carries the tray to the stairs. I know she is waiting, bored and fractious above. I know because she tells me often how she envies me my busy days. Sometimes I want to hate her.

I'm clumsy with my left hand, so although he helped me with the stew, carrying the blue and white tureen up the narrow service stairs to the dining room, and distracts her with small talk at the table, she still notices the limp one. I try not to drip or scald her, not to stain the linen with stock or mess her place setting but there's one too many lumps of potato in the serving spoon and before I can lay them in her dish, it happens — disaster. The stains I can cope with, I've a box of Dolly Blue downstairs for just such things, but the questions I can do without. Especially with him sitting there, watching me squirm, hiding behind his spoon with a smile.

"Careless girl!" She cocks her head to one side, brows furrowing as she considers my deportment. "Why are you holding yourself in such a peculiar way?"

"Please, ma'am, I slipped on the steps this morning and my wrist hasn't been so good since."

Her eyes narrow a little at this. Her husband sputters on his stew, saving me from her further displeasure. He needn't worry; I shan't tell.

"Henry! Sip on your water, dear. You *will* rush your food. Someday you'll choke yourself, and then what will I do?"

I bob my head in curtsey, the 'crisis' over, then escape to the kitchen below. My wrist aches, and I resolve that next time he asks for my hand I'll tell him to have at it himself instead, or ask his wife to do the necessary. He takes so long! It's not worth the money. No wonder she gets bored.

§

Supper is my favourite meal of the day; fresh baked bread with butter and sugar, damson jam in a pot beside, warmed milk and cocoa should Madam want it. Easy to make, easy to serve, and the kitchen smells lovely after. He cuts her two slices and butters them, feeding her small morsels as he sits on the footstool by her feet, feigning romance by the fire as I pour the drinks on the table by the door. Thick warm milk in two thin porcelain cups with a sprinkling of sugar stirred in.

As I turn to pass him his cup I hear her choke. It's a curious noise, like a cough crossed with the noise of a sink draining too fast. Henry sits at her feet and looks bewildered, the whites of his eyes showing all round the circles of brilliant blue.

"Ma'am?! Sir! Oh, dear Lord, help!"

I drop the cup as my lady writhes, and run to the window to call for help. But by the time I have the hooks unfastened and the sash lifted, it is too late and she is purple and still by the fire. He crouches beside her and cries.

"Slut's pennies."

He has shrewd eyes and white lumps protruding from the end of his shiny red nose. I can tell from his breath he had mackerel for breakfast, and from his tone that he doesn't like me at all.

"Beg pardon, sir?"

We're in the kitchen and it doesn't seem like home anymore.

"Slut's. Pennies."

I look at him, seeing white flakes of skin skewered on the stubble round his chin.

"That's what killed your mistress. The doctor cut them out her throat last night."

He watches me sick up something in the sink. I don't know what; I haven't eaten since before supper. My hand shakes as I run the tap to wash it away, and see some neighbours talking outside. They watch me through the window, then turn their backs on the scandal. It's a cold day, especially with the range not lit, but I start to sweat under my pinny, a sour odour wafting round the room.

"So what does that mean? Sir?"

I don't think he's taller than me, but he's broad and I can see from the stripes of darker material at his sides that his uniform's been let out at the seams. He's a little too close to me and I wonder if he's enjoying this.

"It means charges. It means the gaol, and probably you'll hang. As indeed you should."

Snot races the tears to my trembling chin.

"But I didn't do anything!"

He snorts and I wonder if he has a wife or a willing maidservant, and how much he has to pay them.

"*You* are in charge of the kitchen, *you* served supper, *you* gave your mistress under—kneaded bread, *you* let her choke on lumps hard as pebbles within, so how's *that*," he pokes me in the chest with a fat finger, "not doing anything?"

The handcuffs are rough and heavy, and hurt my strained wrist. Henry stands silent and solemn in the hall as the men wrest me out onto the street. I plead with him all the way to the gate:

"Henry, tell them! *You* made the bread, tell them! *Tell* them!"

But no, he can't. Of course, he can't. He can't even meet my eyes.

I think of the scaffold and swallow hard, cursing myself for not doing the same when he came to me that morning, and my mistress for not doing it at all.

An Unusual Darkness

The first thing Jericho Comstock did was grab the hemp rope coiled like an ammonite by his feet and *jump*. Jump high. Jump clear of the towering bulk of the sperm whale's flukes as it crushed the craft and crew that killed it.

Not one of them could swim. But Jericho had the rope and by extension the whale, and decades of whaling had ingrained in him 'you don't got the whale if you don't got the rope'. But perhaps it, the whale, got him.

Salt water scorched his nose, his eyes burned, and the ocean filled his ears with roar. The cold Atlantic shocked him, thickening his joints and numbing his fingers, but as the whale met death in a rage of spray, beating the sea with its tail, he held tight to the thick brown rope, looping it round his wrists in any moment of slack. His hands bound together in and around the rope, as if playing one potato two potato and sticking at just the two, as he often had. The hairy hemp threatened to pull his skin past his knuckles and off like a glove. If the whale went deep he was dead.

They had sighted it early that summer morning, Ernst spotting the distinctive forward forked plume of a sperm whale clearing its lungs. A careless white v frothing into blue sky. Out in the catcher boat, kilometres from the factory ship, the men had eaten their sandwiches, crunched their biscuits, and drunk what they fancied as they rowed closer to the beast. Just as they did most days, the only variety provided by the weather or the mood of the galley staff. A full day's sail away from the parent vessel, they had enough rations to last them a fortnight if they were careful. Sometimes it took that long just to stalk a whale.

All was blue; swelling and rolling, striping dark and pale as the clouds chased birds swooping black against the sky. Sometimes that blue swell rippled when a shark or other unseen predator chased a school of silver to the surface. The men aboard were wary of those ripples; if the boat was too close when the whale sounded they'd be upturned in the instant. If it was a shark below they'd hear the ominous scratches and thumps of investigation beneath their feet and an unease would come upon the crew, short tempers and harsh words spitting between them, Jericho bearing the brunt as always, often not understanding what they meant.

Below the surface, things were bumping his body hard as he hung in the water. He hoped it was just the wreckage. Once something, somebody, clutched at his clothes but its fingers were weak and let go before the face surfaced. Jericho coughed and pedalled his feet to stay afloat. The rope's length away, the great grey beast thrashed in agony, frothing the surface from red to pink as it battered the wreckage of the boat, mashing the bodies within. Jericho vomited as the whale died beside him, returning the seawater from his stomach to its proper place in the crimson sea.

He had lanced it in the Life, the small area behind the jaw that renders the mammoth beast vulnerable to human predators, the swarm of blood vessels nestled under its wrinkled skin inviting his iron. The whale had been about to dive when they took it, the explosion of the bomb–gun thrilling in its brutal noise. He'd tethered the rope, *his* rope, then their boat was skimming the waves as the whale tried to escape them. Jorky and Paul had laughed, enjoying the white–water ride, as Ernst and Carl lanced their prize with more harpoons, taking turns at the bombgun mounted on the side. Blood clouded the water, Jericho looping the excess rope with callused hands as they pulled ever closer to their prey, barely registering its briny scent in the air.

Complacency is a killer, presumption a noose inviting the fatal tug. A swell lifted the boat starboard just as the huge beast arched its back, its tail rising high and dripping through the air. Its black flukes towered over them then smashed down, swatting the catcher, shattering the boat. All around Jericho in the spread of the sea bobbed the remains of his crewmates and the wreckage of their craft, sandwich tins floating in a slew of splintered boards, oars, and Jorky's pale wooden pipe. His ears were ringing, and he could barely hear a sound through the din in his head. The sunshine flared and sparkled off the great corpse beside him. He kicked off his sea boots and toed off his thick woollen socks before their weight could drown him.

Nobody moaned or cried for their mothers. As he shuddered in the water, unwinding the rope from his wrists, as his legs jerked and while he struggled to keep his face dry, a dark grey fin sliced through the mess. A thick yellow jersey he recognised as Paul's rose out of the red soup, a blond head lolling limp to the side. Then a jerk as something claimed the corpse, tugging it silently into the deep.

Something small twitched in the water, just catching his attention from the corner of his eye. Though his glance followed the movement, there was nothing to see. All he could hear was the rasp of his own breathing. His fingers pulsed warm and full as the rope loosened around them. His look darted to the slow swells bobbing him up and down. Shadows that might be from birds slid and darted on or under the water. But the birds were too close to the whale to cast these silhouettes. The sun crept lower at his back, warming his waterlogged hair, and a dark shape slipped long and large below the rope just a metre in front of him.

Watching sleek triangles of charcoal and grey rise and recede through the wreckage as the whale's blood warmed the waters,

Jericho waited for the sharks to notice his pumping legs as, finally, he freed his wrists from the rope. Flexing his fingers, he wrapped the coarse hemp round his right arm before pulling himself, hand by hand, along the cord to the enormous corpse. His harpoon had struck deep and held fast, sharp spurs anchored it within the pale pink flesh. Its eye was small, dark and dull now, fringed with coarse lashes and crusty white growths. It stared at him from death.

This was an old one, older than Jericho by a decade or more. Its skin appeared borrowed from an older, bigger mammal. Thick grey hide hung in wrinkled swatches along its ten−men length. Behind him, Jericho heard something splash the water, close enough to douse his hair with spray. He didn't look back. Scrambling around the firm thickness of flipper, he pulled himself closer to the shaft. It stuck out of the flesh beside him, rope dripping, knot still tight. Something nudged his foot, something with the rasp of sandpaper. He clasped the harpoon with one hand and a fold of whale with the other and hauled up hard.

His body surged from the sea. He scrabbled up the fissured wall of whale as the shark nosed behind him. Pawed the whale's hide for a foothold, a toenail tearing as he did. The birds were shrieking closer, closer.

Only looking up, only seeing the folded grey of salvation, he got a foot on the harpoon shaft and pushed hard against the pole toward safety. His hands clutched, his toes dug into wrinkles. He willed his body up up *up*.

The shark veered away. When he glanced back from where he clung he saw the red stain around his new vessel seething with life, crewmates in pieces he recognised from their clothes, ten or more sharks colliding as they tore at the men and sometimes each other. Creamy birds with pale beaks and sharp cries circled and swooped. One dived to nab a morsel… a snap, was snatched down instead.

His clothes gripped wet upon him. The whale was damp and sticky with blood, its skin rough and dotted with crusty growths of parasites and weed. His feet didn't slip in his climb to the top. Jericho knelt for a moment atop the whale's back, hands anchoring him to its skin. He stared at its warm solidity; red thickening already in the troughs and scars of its skin, patterning the whale like sand at low tide, then raised his pounding head to view the ocean. No sign of smoke or human company on the curve of the horizon. Not another vessel in sight, just clouds beginning to pink and turn orange, the sun descending for someone else's day. Lying flat on his stomach, he crawled to the edge to look back, though every ounce of him wanted to close his eyes and drift away.

The water was churning with tails, fins and teeth, everywhere the teeth, the sea frothing pink as grey and white scythed through the blood, boards and body parts, the creamy heads of unlucky seabirds floating sodden as their companions screeched into the breeze. A smaller shark, narrower than the rest, darted too close to the others, frustrating them. One nipped at the annoyance, turned back to the men... then shifted once more to the casualty with a splash of tail as it writhed in agony, purpled guts spilling free in tight loops of tubing. More red bloomed around the frenzy, hanging in the ocean, stirring the fish to ever more excitement.

Someone's hand bobbed pale and ignored beside the great mass of whale.

Jericho wasn't so bothered about the details of his crewmates' death; living on a whaler, death is a daily event, be it of fish caught for dinner, a cat crushed under a barrel, crew falling ill, or a whale that didn't get away. But he minded about his own. His whole body clenched as he watched the too-close turmoil below, until the pain of his buckling fingernails registered and he released his grip just a little; not enough to slip. He couldn't fail to notice that his own whale was sinking. The folds he'd clambered up first were now submerged beneath the roiling red water. Great grey snouts bumped at the corpse, rising from the bloody stew, one flashing its belly white above the water as it bit

78

and rolled, pulling a trousered leg away from its twin, tussling with a fellow feeder. Another tore a chunk from the flipper, eating away at his safety.

Transferring the rope, shifting it − 'you don't got the whale if you don't got the rope' − to his other hand Jericho squirmed on his belly to the middle of the head. The puncture of blowhole slopped with thick ruby soup, a fountain subsiding as the unlikely vessel shifted in the swells of a shark nudged sea, bubbles rising through the blood as its lungs relaxed in death, its carcass deflating beneath his feet. There was nothing but pink clouds on the curved blue wall of horizon, and nothing but death for Jericho below. Raising his arm he formed his aching fingers into a fist. Punching deep into the blowhole of the beast, a gush of blood spurted up around his elbow, spraying him with gore, bright lit in the track of the sun on the horizon. It was over his clothes and hair; he smelled rich tangy copper − the scent of a good day's work for a whaler. Manna for sharks. His arm was hot. He held it straight, stoppering the lungs. A plug of flesh that kept this particular whale afloat. Watched the sun creep closer to the horizon. Soon night must fall.

Trapped, isolated, exhausted, Jericho watched the birds scream and swoop around him, fighting over a finger or remnant of thigh, and allowed his eyes to drift shut. The wreckage was sinking and dispersing. He was shuddering with cold. Rescue was out of the question.

A bird landed close to his feet. Pecked a toe.

He kicked at it, drew his legs beneath him, and remembered home. It wasn't a good memory. But it was all he had.

An Unusual Darkness is the first chapter in Gill's forthcoming novel of the same name.

NON-FICTION

Creating a stink

It's not like I was asking them to kill one for me. I wouldn't. I *like* whales. But as I made 'phone call after 'phone call, my little boy playing at my feet with bin lorries and bottle tops, I got the impression the people I was contacting thought there was something weird about this.

I write, and even though I write a lot of fiction, sometimes several short stories a day, and spin tall tales at bedtime for my four year old, it's important to me to base it all in reality. The most successful lies are those spun through with truth.

Especially when it comes to describing the basest of facts: the sensual details of physical reactions. If I'm writing about someone in a bakery, I want to know what it smells like — if the batter mix heating in the oven wafts a sickly eggy—sugar—butter stink through the prep area or if there's a charred stench from the drips and spatters burning on the bottom.

I want to know if the more fashion conscious in there have fringes flopping down over their faces when they're outside taking a break, hair nets off, bangs cut in just to hide the itchy red line left across their foreheads by the elastic. I want to know how long it takes to become sick of the taste of cake—mix, to stop wanting to lick the spoon at the end of the batch or clean the bowls of icing with the tip of a tongue.

I want to know if their hands are soft or stinging by the end of the day. If they've given up on pretty rings and manicures. I want to know it all.

So now that I'm writing a book, my third, about a man stuck in (and on) the rotting corpse of a whale, I have a lot of questions. Yes, I know it will stink. But there is a whole palette of stench out there. I *have* to know more.

A sperm whale has washed up, several days dead, on a golden stretch of sand in Skegness, a single day's travel away from my twitching nostrils. As I wipe my son's face after a particularly messy breakfast of French toast, my mind is full of whale.

A train to Glasgow then several connections and a taxi – and I'd be in sniffing distance. But I can't get childcare, and as my husband has started a new job, this seemingly fated encounter of writer and whale just isn't going to happen. I consider, very briefly, taking my son with me, remember his boredom and agitation on the 50 minute journey to Glasgow, extrapolate this out to about 15 hours, watch him happily playing with his toys, and decide against it.

A couple of phone calls to bemused officials and the news–desk of the local paper and I discover that the carcass has been shrouded in a yellow mountain of sand. They're waiting on a licence to come through to let them tow it out to sea and get rid of it. Till then, it stinks and is drawing scavengers, so several tonnes of sand should help preserve their tourist trade.

"Do you know if anyone kept any scraps in a jar?"

"Er, no. No, I'm not aware of anyone doing *that*."

"Would anyone be able to collect me some? I'd pay for the postage and costs. Or even just some of the sand it's leaked onto, the smelly bits. I just need to smell it."

A pause.

"Let me see if someone else can help you with this…"

It's a pass–the–parcel of bemusement and disbelief.

Nobody owns up to keeping even the merest sliver of whale or spoonful of stinking sand. Nobody, not a one. I find that very hard to believe. There's bound to be some school kid or antisocial neighbour with at least a little bit of the beast hidden in their mum's freezer. But not even a plea for help through the local newspaper produces fruit.

"Hi – I was wondering if you knew whether anyone collected any samples from the whale on the beach?"

"Er – what?"

"Or if you could run an appeal for them on my behalf? Just in case?"

"Sure, of *course*. Why not? Let me just take some details…"

Two months later, there's still not a word about it on their site.

I could read what others have written; compose my own story using second or third hand olfactory experiences of smells long forgotten. But I'd *much* rather experience the stench of rotting whale flesh for myself.

The corpse is soon dragged away, the tide sluicing the shore clean and allowing the locals to breathe deep once again, nothing but exhaust fumes and salt air on the wind. I give up on this particular perfect whale, and start emailing my friends: "Anybody know what dead whale smells of? Anybody have a marine biologist friend who might have a sample in a fridge I could sniff?"

And eventually came the surprising response – durian fruit.

Durian fruit.

None in the supermarkets or on the greengrocer's stall. Some airlines ban them, their smell is just too pungent. I wonder if they're ever imported here?

"Anybody know where I can get hold of some durian fruit?"

Protein

The market stank of blood and bleach, the lights were fluorescent and flickering, the tiles brown and grouted with grime, but as I came upon the dangling pheasants, I was home.

We moved to a fishing village when I was about ten years old, much against my will, and a middle–aged couple agreed to babysit my sister and I while my mother worked. Mr and Mrs were soon Aunt and Uncle, honorary but binding just the same. Uncle Jim was and is a hunting/shooting/fishing practical man, and I had been raised only in towns until the latest move to the country. It was a shock to all our systems, but a good one.

We went out in a boat once to check the creels for lobsters and season the vessel, and I remember the blue of the sky, the salt tang of the ocean, and the coastline shrinking from sight as water flooded my trainered feet and I bailed us out with a beaker. The ribs of the boat were dry and narrowed from a winter on shore, and required time at sea to swell them for a neater, watertight fit. Logical, but terrifying for a child who had recently watched 'Jaws'.

The lobsters were speckled a deep navy blue, and rattled about the bucket, climbing each other to wave their claws at us. We made it back to the harbour without incident, but my dreams were of drowning that night. The lobsters went with their bucket to my Aunt Jean's kitchen, and I escaped into the vegetable garden, smelled fresh turned earth and parsley, and peered in the shed.

Weathered brown wood loomed at the top of the garden path. In south west Scotland, the flat areas are mainly fields or beach. The garden sloped up to a summit of shed and the earwiggy logpile Papa sawed for the fire inside. The door was always locked, the small window grey with cobwebs and snail trails. I'd stand on my tiptoes and peer in. Deep with shadows, I could never see more than the outlines of mysterious tools and items within.

Then one day I saw inside.

I can only compare it to the old tale of Bluebeard and the blood–stained key and his many headless wives. Past the workbench and coffee jars of screws, pins and nails, beside the wooden handled spades and fork, dangled blood spattered birds. Bunches of them, open beaked and broken necked, heavy in death. Partridge, pheasants, and grouse, dark red dribbles on their ugly grey legs, eyelids rolled up, some half open, bald and pink. I was horrified, sickened... but fascinated too. These birds were so secretive, so dainty as they scurried about the fields behind my Uncle's house. Aside from the occasional tattered mat of roadkill, I'd never seen them up close.

Fingering feathers, I noticed movement beneath a dappled beige breast. The beak was yellow, dirty, and half open in silent squawk. Its eye was dull and dusty. The bird was unquestionably dead.

It was maggots.

My uncle explained the birds had to hang till the meat was tender, and the flesh loosed its grip on the fatal pellets. Sometimes, creatures squirmed in their wake. Just a wee bit of protein, nothing that would harm you, all adding to the flavour.

My Uncle Jim and Aunt Jean are rare cooks, and twenty years later I still yearn for their soup, stews, and fire toasted bread. I'm also vegetarian.

Black Fish

"The water which supports a boat can also sink it."

Chinese proverb.

Whether you've found a body or not, when you grow up in a fishing village you soon associate its blue–grey neighbour with death and disappointment. Even the happiest of memories have salt water as a backdrop; in the sad ones, you tear up in sympathy. The Kennedy Park, flatly green above the Firth of Clyde, lures tourists of all ages with its stubborn grey castle, toilets and views. Family fun days had wobbly stalls, an unspoken etiquette, and village games when I was young there. Football. Rounders. Tug of war with shopkeepers and fishermen, sunburn, smiles and banter. Mr Edgar's orange hair glossy as he hauled the white rag over the line on the grass, ruddy forearms used to winching silver harvests on board the *Copia* whatever the weather. People fell laughing on the lumpy football pitch by the stonecast toilet block. His son stood by with his friends, the teenagers apart from the rest of us, enjoying in parallel as near–adults do.

Then, ten days before Christmas, there was a problem on board the fishing boat. Mr Edgar and his partner made for port. A storm blew up, the boat went down, and two children were left without a father in Dunure. Lost at sea. Never coming home.

I would see orange hair bobbing along the shingled shore, heading north past Fisherton, the next hamlet along. Lost buoys and wreaths of seaweed and sky—blue rope lay tangled on the beach, with eyes of pink ringed agate nestled beneath.

Dunure is renowned for its Saturn ringed stones and geodes with tiny crystal caves hidden within. I had field trips from school there, lots of discussion on the rocks poured from the long dead volcano across the water, the twinkling quartz crystals, the sand, shells and stones. Ailsa Craig was all that remained of it, a volcanic plug covered in birds far out to sea, like the cork left when a wine bottle shatters, or the burnt—on crust of a pie amongst the washing up. That half—orphaned boy seemed oblivious to the beauty. Whether sunny or snow, there was always shadow on his face. Sometimes his friends helped in the search, clusters of them disturbing the oystercatchers with their mourning feathers and peep—peep—peep.

A loner, I walked the walk too, paperbacks in my pockets, a drink in my hand. Who lost this rope? Or this shoe, or this boot? Did he drink from this shard of mug, or crumple this empty crisp packet? The birds would skitter beside me, while the sheep cropped grass above. I avoided the others, and the only mammal's body I found was a cow.

I had walked quite far, past the holiday camp of Butlin's, to the surge of land jutting high above the sea, seeming paused before an inevitable *crash*. Grey pebbles scrunched and slipped below my trainers. I paused to draw a mermaid using a stick in a golden patch of sand. Moved toward the bigger rocks, hoping for rock pools. Amongst some grey boulders draped with dry seaweed flung there in a long calmed storm were the back legs of a cow. They seemed slender and dainty in death, hooves poking up at the enormous sky, dwarfed by the height of the craggy Heads of Ayr.

Big black crows hopped about. Most of its carcass lay obscured. I smelled salt air and drying seaweed. Heard the ssshhh of the gentle sea, the popping of gorse seeds, and the activity of the crows. I focussed on the splashes of lichen on the rocks nearby, yellow and orange and greeny–white. Signs of good, clean air this cow would no longer breathe. Leaving the crows to their feast, I watched the tide turn, saw it change its mind and edge closer to the beast. It seemed longer, going home.

Fishing, though nothing like it used to be, is still a major industry here, the salt blood in Scotland's veins. Less than 8.6% of the UK's population lives here yet nearly two thirds of British fish are landed at its ports. It takes its toll, and not just on the fish. Yet it continues, lucky fathers passing their knowledge and gear on to their sons, and the idea of being grounded on land for good strikes terror in many a man's heart. The coast has its own culture, its own traditions and beliefs. Women are seen as unlucky. So are swans, some boats won't even have the matches on board – though we usually had a pair in the harbour at Dunure, for tourists to feed and sailors to tut over.

And I remember a summer, after the *Copia*, with pink skies and short nights, and jellyfish stinking on the shore. Mooching round the harbour, watching the boils of anemones in the rockpools by the lighthouse flowering then feasting. Envying the pleasure boats throttling out; escaping. A few handsome young men having a drink in the sun, gathered outside the pub that awaited the sailors' safe return. Light glittered off the harbour's water. Where the damply barnacled walls shadowed it, you could see crabs sidling about, empty shells skeleton white, and seaweed furring up the creel lines. Somehow we got chatting; about the sea, the summer, and what you could do around here. Paul, or Wicksey as he was known to many, reminded me of pictures of David Essex I'd seen in my mum's old annuals. Curly brown hair past a silver–hooped ear, eyes that made you go 'oh!' – if you were a crush prone teenager. Always a smile.

He shocked me. Told me lots of sailors don't bother learning to swim. If it's their time, why prolong it? Fishing is a cold, sometimes solitary pursuit round here. If your boat goes down, well, where are you going to go? If you fall in, either you're lucky and a crewmate fishes you out, or you're not.

Apart from the safety stuff, my jaw dropped at the thought of living on this beautiful coast, with summer warmed water and plenty of rocks to swim to and explore, walking to the edge, and saying 'no'. True, there was a sewage pipe that meant you had to choose your tides wisely, but it just seemed like such a waste. Later, I married a man with summer sea eyes, and heard similar stories from his uncle, non—swimmer and lucky survivor of the sunken *Empire Spruce*. We moved away to a land—locked town in England, and walk the shores with each return, our little boy in tow.

But between that, between the leaving and the marrying, Paul became a hero.

The fish are in trouble: too many are taken, too many are lost. It feels like for every link in the silver meshed dredge there's a rule with numbers, brackets and dots to tell you who and how and when and where, until your bank gets cross and the sea beckons escape.

Shaun Ritchie, 27, was married with two sons, a fisherman with family responsibilities and costly ambition. He bought a boat, the *Equinox*, and sent her for refitting as a clam dredger. After, the welder who'd done the work with him said he wasn't an expert on boats, but thought the equipment looked "very heavy for the size of the boat". With her nose trimmed, the vessel was under twelve metres long. That way, she didn't have to meet the full safety regulations. Investigators doubted she'd have passed the 'roll test'.

91

As a dredger, the *Equinox* needed winching gear for hoisting up the dredge and a heavily reinforced hull for the half–tonne of catch Shaun was hoping for. Usually this gear is fitted at the rear of the boat, the bow being able to balance the weight and pressure well in a small vessel whose size makes her more susceptible to rolling over and capsizing in the waves. But Shaun had the gear moved to allow the catch to be winched over the side of the boat instead. Burdened with the added weight, when she was returned to Ayr harbour she rode very low in its calm water, with just a few inches between its still grey surface and the deck. People commented on this to Shaun, officials and sailors alike, but he reckoned she handled well...

The *Equinox* usually required a crew of two, Shaun and 19 year old Darren White, but when Shaun had little luck with his catches due to ill weather, a plan was formed that saw five aboard the butchered boat.

Paul, 28, was now living with Pamela Crossan, also 28, and her 6 year old, Kayleigh, just along the street from the late Mr. Edgar. Kayleigh had gone to Stranraer for a holiday down the coast with her grandparents, so on the night of Saturday 25th May 1996, Paul and Pamela were enjoying a few drinks in a bar by Ayr harbour. His boat, the *Constant Grace*, was tied up there for the weekend as legislation meant the fleet couldn't work the Firth of Clyde from midnight on Friday to midnight on Sunday. A prawn fisherman and doting stepfather, Paul and his beloved Pamela were trying for a baby together.

It was a lovely night, the weather had turned, and Shaun was apparently desperate to recoup the cost of his boat's conversion. Pamela and Paul had never been on the *Equinox* before but joined him and Darren with Derek Bryden, 20, Paul's usual crewmate. Paul's big brother, Bill, a harbour official at Ayr, had no idea he'd gone out. To fish off the books, for 'black fish' as they call it, meant risking a £5,000 fine. But Paul was a lovely guy, who'd do anything for anyone, and happy–go–lucky besides. With Kayleigh taken care of for the night it was a chance to show Pamela the beauty and reality of what he did every day on the *Constant Grace*.

They sailed south at about ten o'clock that night, the Isle of Arran to the right, the Heads of Ayr jutting to their left, the beam dredging clams and their natural predators from the mud at the bottom of the Firth. It's chillier at sea. Paul lent Pamela his leather jacket, and she sheltered in the wheelhouse.

The dredge had trailed behind the *Equinox* like the train of a wedding dress, collecting clams not confetti below their white frothed wake. Unlike a car, the engine of a fishing boat has a whole vocabulary of noises, not just a growl. If a car has the velvety ribbon of purr, the boat has a rosary of small explosions. The smells of fuel and salt sea life were a far remove from the warm bar they'd left not long before. Pamela was insulated from the noise somewhat in the draughty wheel house, Derek by her side, but it still made conversation difficult.

The guys started winching up the heavy metal cables, bringing their catch to the surface, hoping for plenty of clams rather than empty shells and octopus. Metal, rope, and cable turned and strained and struggled, released a shrieking groan. The seabed shelves in that area, and there are plenty of underwater cables, wreckage and junk to snag the beam as it rakes the murk for clams. It's part of the work, like farmers snagging their plough in a root strewn field. When it happens, you fix the fouled line, you jiggle the dredge free, you sort it somehow or lose the catch.

But then the dredge somehow caught and a cable snapped under the pressure. Already unstable, already straining with the winching, the *Equinox* leaned closer to the sea. The water that slopped onto the deck had no escape. The scuppers, those gaps along the side that let splashes reunite with the sea, had been blocked. Hatches were jammed. It all served to weigh the *Equinox* down. The crew had to fight to maintain their balance on the slippery slanting deck. Paul climbed the metal rigging to clear the broken line but his weight shifted the balance further. Derek, watching from the wheelhouse with Pamela, said to her:

93

"I don't like the look of this,"

and ran out on deck. As the *Equinox* turned inevitably into the cold black water, the men jumped overboard. Pamela found herself trapped in the wheelhouse. The door jammed. The boat sinking. No way out. Which way was up? Which way to go? Time slowing in the terror, as if stopping to watch the accident in progress.

Somehow she escaped. A passionate swimmer, winning medals for it in her youth, she swam to the surface. When Paul saw her, he shouted:

"C'mon Pamela, c'mon babes!"

She couldn't breathe. Sudden immersion in cold water does that to you, it literally takes your breath away. She clung to the sinking vessel. There were no life buoys on board and nothing else for her to hang onto. The old tyres looped to the sides with rope acted as bumpers in port, protected the boat from scrapes and bumps against walls and other vessels: there was no way to get them off in a hurry. Paul shouted:

"Get away from the boat!"

knowing she would go down with it if she kept clinging on. He held her up, kept saying:

"C'mon babes – deep breaths – keep calm. Let's get some of those heavy clothes off you,"

told her to take off his jacket. It was dragging her down.

The pleasant evening had given way to a cold, clear night. Stars sparkling, sea beautiful but deadly, with a line of orange and white lights bordering the coast on either side, tantalising but reinforcing the reality of their mile and a half separation from dry land.

None of them wore lifejackets; fishermen find them too bulky and expensive, with a tendency to get caught in the gear. On a calm sea, capsize seems impossible. The boat went down too fast for a Mayday call to go out. With it being the weekend, there were no vessels nearby to offer help.

Shaun took charge, said they should stick together, tried to calm the boys, but to no avail. With seventy feet of water below their shivering legs, and the younger lads panicking, Pamela disobeyed the skipper and made the only decision she could. Knowing their last hope was help from the shore, she decided to swim the mile and a half home.

She was panicking too, but just kept thinking:

"I can't drown. It was so horrible... I had gone right under with the boat and I *knew* drowning must be the most awful way to die."

Unlike most modes of death, many have died from drowning then been successfully resuscitated. These lucky souls describe a terrible burning sensation, then complete peace. Calm.

Then nothing.

It reminds me of descriptions of drinking raw whisky. I hope it was no worse.

Pamela never once looked back. Just started swimming.

"I thought the others would follow me, but then I heard singing. It was Paul and Shaun... singing their daft songs... they must have been singing to try and keep the boys' spirits up. It was awful."

With such a way to go through the cold flat surface of the sea, it was as if she was staying still.

"At first I seemed to be getting nowhere and I was no closer to the shore."

As hours went by, the sea grew quiet except for her splashing and gasping in the 8C water.

"All I could think was that Paul wasn't going back to sea on Monday. He could just stay at home."

She was terrified, cold, and numb. The closer she got to the lights of the Butlin's camp, the more she called for help. But nobody heard.

Then, just after 1.15am, Alastair Dick was sitting in a caravan with his fiancée and her mum, down for a holiday from Glasgow.

"I heard screams saying 'Help me, help me, *please* help me now!'"

He called security then followed the voice toward the shore, joining three other holiday—makers there, who had also heard her plight.

"We couldn't see anything so we shouted to the woman to keep shouting so we could try to find her. We crossed the fence and went onto the beach and saw her in about three feet of water."

Wading out into the cold cold water, they helped Pamela to shore.

"She could not move at all or feel any part of her body. We took our clothes off and wrapped them round her to give her some warmth. Through the chittering we were able to make out that the fishing boat had capsized... four men were missing. I went back into the water to see if I could locate any more, but I couldn't find any."

She had made it. Rushed to the medical centre, then hospital, Pamela was treated for hypothermia, exhaustion, and a chest infection. Doctors there were amazed, calling it:

"A triumph, equal to climbing Mount Everest on one leg without oxygen."

She had been in the darkly drowning water for nearly four hours.

The coastguard, lifeboats and police scrambled with others for a search of the area. The boys were found floating near where the boat had gone down. Shaun washed up five weeks later. Paul remains lost to this day. Only Pamela survived.

Bill Blaikie, still on duty at the port, only knew his little brother was lost at sea once Pamela was rescued from the shallows of the cold night shore. It fell to him to make the call that every parent, and sibling, dreads.

§

So the legislation changed. Pamela is still a heroine. The men are still dead.

Paul is still lost, and a hero.

And I go home with my family, walk along the shingle with its smooth blond patches of sand, walk along, and listen.

Prospects

At ten months, babies can usually sit, crawl, and stand. They babble and coo and play games with people who catch their eye. They cannot, however, save lives. Not theirs, nor anyone else's.

The boy sprawled on the deck of the sinking *Tayleur* was helpless, sodden, and cold – an orphan dependent on the kindness of strangers. 147 other children were already dead, crushed against the rocks by thick grey waves and debris, sucked under by their heavy layers of clothes, or drowned as they lay prone with seasickness in their cabins below. A man – French or German, and braver than brave – saw him lying there as saltwater sluiced the deck. He was one of the last to attempt escape, and had just stripped down to his shirt as he made the unenviable choice between a swim to shore through the bodies and brains of those who hadn't made it, the incoming tide crashing heavy wooden spars and boxes against the swimmers and the rocks, or the rope hanging between the sinking ship and those who'd *just* survived.

Pulling himself along the rope, the fibres raw and coarse against his palms, he looked back and saw the infant, alone. Alive. Grabbing it, he clenched the back of its clothing between his teeth and inched his way over the thick grey surf to the rocks, then tied the child to his back with clothing and began the climb up near vertical cliffs to safety above.

They were very, very lucky.

§

The *Tayleur* was built at breakneck speed over the course of 6 months in the redbrick town of Warrington, England. She was a hotchpotch of mistakes and making do, an iron hulled steamer converted to clipper status, with ill−positioned masts and a rudder too small to make much of a difference to her steering at sea. These were just some of the causes blamed at the inquest just a few months later, when she should still have been on her way to the gold rush.

Her size is hard to imagine: 230 feet long, 40 feet across, with three masts and three decks, and holds 28 feet below deck. 4,000 tons of cargo could be carried in her, and her loads were unusual even for the time. There was a piano, blank gravestones for ballast, prefabricated houses, Welsh roof slates, bricks, and a small steamboat lashed onto the deck, for use on an Australian river. Its engineer and his wife lived in its cabin for the duration of the voyage, meant for Melbourne but cut short by an island a couple of miles off the Irish coast. The total value of the estimated cargo was about £20,000, over a million in today's prices. Very little of that was insured, but there were few left afterwards to whom that mattered.

Only the upper deck was used for passengers, the lower two reserved for cargo and crew. Much was made of the crew, after. But how much was prejudice, and how much true, is hard to judge from modern reading.

A ship of the *Tayleur*'s tonnage was required by the Emigration Commissioners to carry a crew of 60 seamen: she had an inexperienced complement of 37 − plus 23 stewards − engaged the week before they sailed. Of these, the captain knew only two, the third mate and the carpenter. Although it was widely reported that the crew was mainly foreign and unable to comprehend the captain's instructions, in the official report only two were found to have no working knowledge of the English language. Less widely reported was the reaction of the islanders when one of the ship's cooks made it up the cliff and ran for help. He was a black man, most likely the first they'd ever seen. They shut their doors on him and hid. Lack of comprehension cut both ways.

The *Tayleur*'s captain, 29 year—old John Noble of Penrith, was an experienced sailor of the England — Australia route, engaged specifically because of his expertise. He fell from the forecastle into her main hold while she was under construction, leaving him shaken and unable to join the ship as she surged into the River Mersey. Another accident on board left a man with his tongue "divided into three or four parts", and Charles Tayleur, whose foundry made the ship, did not attend the launch on 4th October 1853 as his wife had died but a few days earlier.

Despite these ill—starred events, there was a celebratory atmosphere as at 1.25pm the *Tayleur* came free of the chocks, a large crowd gathering to watch and cheer from the riverbanks despite the grim weather. Shops closed early for the day, the river's level rose and soaked many of the onlookers, and a reporter for the *Warrington Guardian* rather bitchily reported: "men guiltless of a bath before, now undergoing the 'water cure'… It was a most amusing thing to see delicate ladies, and brawny men, and even policemen, who were there to keep the ground, not being able to keep their own, but with hands aloft, and boots be—bogged, at last running from a danger they had never *apprehended.*"

More touchingly, he wrote: "whilst the hammers still rang their loudest, old gentlemen reverted to the habits of boyhood, and clambered across poles, and up ladders, balanced themselves on timbers, hung on by coping—stones, and showed all the glee imaginable at the lively character of the event."

A local politician's daughter christened the ship with a bottle of wine, red ribbons fluttering in the breeze, and an unusually high tide helped the vessel glide smoothly into the water. Three tugs guided it to Liverpool for provisioning, the *Tayleur* banging into one of them on the way with such force that the smaller vessel was shunted up onto the bank and had to be pushed off by some men working on a railway line close by, sparking rumours of her 'luck'.

Still, the crowds gathered once again. Notices were posted round the docks on 10th January to tell the passengers to be aboard for the 14th. For many of those on board, it would be the last time they ever set foot on dry land.

Three were very lucky, though they didn't know it at the time. A mother and child were pronounced unfit for the voyage and returned to port, and an Irish passenger got confused when the steam tug *Victory* took the office clerks and friends of those on board away, and jumped aboard thinking there was something wrong. It was getting dark, and they were quite far away from the *Tayleur* when someone saw him standing on a paddle box and said to him "Come down out of that." He replied "Where are we going?" and when they told him "Liverpool" he seemed dreadfully confused, and said he wanted to go to Melbourne. They turned the steamboat about and tried to catch up, but she outpaced them, and they had to return to Liverpool instead. He only had what he stood up in, all his clothes and possessions were still on board the *Tayleur* – but he lived.

Once the *Victory* was well away, five stowaways were discovered. The *Tayleur* was a luxury ship for well–to–do emigrants, hoping for better lives and greater social mobility in the gold fields of Australia, well away from the overcrowded squalor of a cholera–ridden England and a starving Ireland. In theory, the stowaways chose well.

Ireland was a country dependent on the potato both for sustenance and animal fodder in the mid–1800s. Increasingly, fields were used to raise crops and animals for export, leaving little but potatoes as an option for the working class. This monoculture was a recipe for disaster with an ingredient of one; when blight was added to the mix, the fields yielded a grey sludge of rot that meant starvation and fatal susceptibility to diseases for over a million people in just five years. The landowners were still able to export shipfuls of corn and cattle, so to some it was not a 'famine' but a deliberate cull of the poor. Controversially, some recent historians have gone so far as to call it 'Ireland's holocaust'.

Those who could fled to Scotland, England, Canada, America… whoever would take them, wherever they could go. In the receiving countries, the rich muttered about overcrowding, the poor about competition for jobs. Those feeling the pressure but able to afford the chance of a new life in the sun, digging for gold or making money from those who did, were emigrating by the shipload. Thousands turned up to the so-called Tent Cities, proper accommodation being hard to find due to the sheer number of people arriving every day.

The *Tayleur* held gold diggers, sailors, inn keepers, clerks, farmers, miners, and artisans. There were families and singletons, friends, masters and servants. The ship's surgeon, Dr. R. Hannah Cunningham, was a young Scot, hale and hearty and enthusiastic about the voyage now underway. He had every reason to be optimistic about the welfare of those in his care – including his wife and their infant son, Henry, as they looked forward to their new life in Melbourne, Australia.

The comparative opulence and luxury of the *Tayleur* was at odds with the squalor and stink of the transportation ships with their cargo of prisoners. She was described as "an amazing vessel and the workmanship in her is throughout of the very best description… she is only fitted for about three-quarters the number which she is capable of carrying, the remaining space being liberally given up by her owners to increase the accommodation afforded… She is also very lofty and her ventilation is perfect. A shaft through her foregallant deck and four portholes in her stern afford a constant current of air through the ship and she has besides seven covered hatchways with windows to open and close, and sidelights about eight inches apart, along her whole length and opening into every berth...

In every respect the *Tayleur* is the perfect model of what an emigrant ship ought to be for such a voyage to Australia. No expense has been spared in her construction, or in her fitting—up; it can scarcely be doubted that she will prove herself worthy of the great skill, pains and liberal expense which have been bestowed on her."

And poignantly, "no vessel ever left this port with fairer prospects of a successful and pleasant journey than the *Tayleur*, which was amply proved by the cheering on board as she passed down the river, and the excellent spirits which prevailed amongst them."

Soon seasickness would cause many to take to their berths. Most would not leave them again.

The pilot, who left them just past the island of Anglesey, praised her handling, saying after, "I took the *Tayleur* to sea on Thur. last, the ship being in the tow of the steam tug *Victory*. While the wind was light, the steamship continued towing her, but as soon as the breeze sprung up the steamer was obliged to drop astern, as such were the sailing qualities of the ship that she would have run over the steamer. During the passage down I had full opportunity to examine the compasses and found half a point difference between the compasses below and those upon deck. The ship answered her helm and steered like a fish; I do not hesitate to state that I believed her to be the fastest ship afloat."

The iron hull that meant this ship could be bigger, better, faster, also meant the compasses didn't work. Captain Noble, under pressure with a new boat, new and inexperienced crew, and under—stretched ropes that made using the sails a time—consuming liability, failed to check and calibrate the compasses on the river or as they left the Mersey for the Irish Sea. The weather turned dirty as the tug left them, and it was harder to see. Sails flapped and canvas tore, the ship raced through rough seas, and those passengers with experience of sea travel grew wary.

Michael Reidy of Galway, told the inquest: "At about 4 o'clock on the Friday morning, I was lying in my berth with my clothes on, when a passenger named Holland told me that there was great confusion on board and that if any accident occurred I would have the best chance of saving myself by being on deck. When I got on deck I observed the greatest confusion and very few hands on deck, and I observed one of the sails on the mainmast torn, and all the sails flapping about. I saw no exertions made aloft to reef them or take them in. Two sailors were hauling a rope near the mainmast and I went to assist them. I did so because I saw there was great necessity.

"Captain Noble came up in the meantime and asked one of the sailors what they were doing. The man told him, and he seemed satisfied. I was then assisting in hauling the rope. The captain went four or five yards along the deck when the man he had addressed followed him and complained of two men he had found lashed on the cradle asleep. The captain said if he caught them asleep they would recollect it. I remarked to the captain that the passengers felt greatly disappointed at the crew; the more so on account of their having had confidence in him that he would not have gone to sea with such hands. The captain said, 'I knew no more what they were than you did. They engaged themselves in Liverpool as good and efficient men, and I had no opportunity of knowing what they were until now, when I find that they are not efficient, and indifferent as they are, they have gone down and hid themselves among the passengers and can't be found'."

Out of a crew of 70, the Captain knew only the carpenter and the third mate, beforehand. At the inquest, the third mate said: "As far as I saw the crew and had them under my charge they were a good and efficient crew." But then, at the inquest, there was more going on than met the eye.

§

In 1851, Edward Hargraves struck gold on a site he called Ophir, near Bathurst in New South Wales, Australia. Thousands begged, borrowed, saved and stole to get there, hiding aboard ships, working their passage, agreeing to jobs then absconding to the diggings on arrival, just for the chance of a fortune in a foreign land. Most of the arrivals camped out in the Tent Cities, putting a strain on services and supplies, and providing another source of income and employment to the emigrants so keen to escape Great Britain. 41,491 emigrants sailed just from Liverpool in 1854.

One such group was the Griffiths family of Herefordshire, England. Charles and Sarah ran the Bull's Head Inn on Widemarsh Common, in the small market town of Holmer. Sarah's mother and sister lived just a few miles away in Ross, and generally, those who lived there, stayed there. But, just months after the birth of their son, Arthur, the three left for Liverpool and the comforts of the *Tayleur*. Sarah's mother remained, tending gardens for others as she awaited news of their safe voyage; an unusual occupation for a woman of that era. Things would get stranger still.

On board the *Tayleur*, the ropes were stiff and unstretched, the sails untended, the compass readings a lie, and the weather getting dirtier by the hour. Captain Noble, who neither changed his clothes nor slept from the day the vessel left Liverpool to the moment it ran against rocks "as black as death" less than two days later, strode the deck as visibility grew poorer and passengers with experience of sailing assisted with hauling in ropes and reefing the sails, greasing blocks too small for the ropes to pass through easily, a sense of unease spreading amongst the more knowledgeable on board.

Those unused to the constant movement of the ocean were mainly confined to their berths, seasick and not caring whether they lived or died, even when their cabin—mates ran to tell them of the looming rocks. A stomach churning mixture of nausea and vertigo caused by the confusion of signals to the brain as the body moves and the eyes seem to show all is still, it can last for hours or days, and vomiting barely helps.

The air was grey and foggy, the iron hull coping well with the choppy waves, as deep currents in the Irish Sea drew the *Tayleur* off course. The compasses couldn't show it. Captain Noble didn't take soundings at any point in the 47—hour voyage, a fact that drew castigation from those serving on the inquests later, and scorn from the press. An experienced and well—respected captain, he made odd mistakes on this voyage. Lack of sleep may explain his lapses in judgement, but didn't make it any easier for the bereaved to forgive them.

This was the *Titanic* of its day; a glamorous well—publicised maiden voyage of an enormous ship, flying the White Star's flag as it left for foreign shores, sinking in unusual circumstances with a largely avoidable and shocking loss of life. It was not insured for nearly its worth, and with the bad press and failed investments the name of the line, the company, and its ensign were soon sold on – to Thomas H. Ismay, father of Bruce Ismay of *Titanic* fame.

The wreck was rediscovered in 1957 after local fishermen's comments about lobster caught in the area attracted the attention of a local diving club. Apparently, the usually dark blue lobsters were coming on board with red undersides, as if they had been living on something rusty. Something big.

The plates of the hull had long since collapsed into the sediment, but the wreck is in shallow water and divers found the ship's bell, pinnacle, portholes, brass dog collars, salt in jars, boots, shoes, cosmetics, and a wealth of other items besides, though the gold sewn into women's corsets and held in the passengers' cabins is lost – either to the sand or persons unknown. Counterfeit money and fool's gold lurk in the sand, whoever they belonged to probably lost along with them. There was so much blue and white Staffordshire crockery found that a sale was held at the end of Rogerstown pier on the mainland, as despite its age and history, it was held to be near enough worthless, though some has remained in museums as mundane relics of the past.

The wreck is classed as a heritage site; permission must be granted for a dive, and it is one of the most visited wrecks of the area. Footage of its anemones, lobsters, and edible crabs with black tipped claws can be viewed online, along with the starfish decorating the unmarked headstones lying like toppled dominos in the murky green.

Five watertight compartments meant that had the *Tayleur* struck rocks head–on, she'd likely have been saved. The thick haze and foul weather prevented them taking observations all of Friday. Lights were passed in the night then land was spotted at about ten the next morning, but there was no indication of where that land was – and what lay about it. An hour and a half later, a lookout shouted "Breakers on the starboard bow!"

Having attempted to stop the ship from grounding on the rocks by letting out both anchors, the cables "snapping like twine" as the weather forced them on against their will, Captain Noble "kept the headyards braced full, for the purpose of swinging her in broadside to the rocks, so as to give the passengers a chance of getting off. We made no attempt to lower the boats; they would not be able to live in the sea. We had eight aboard, including the steamboat."

He allowed the strong tide to run the ship breadthways against the rocks between Seal Hole and the Nose of Lambay, an island just north of Dublin. The one boat they let down smashed in an instant, adding to the debris in the water.

A survivor later told the inquest: "It was then blowing heavily, and a high sea running... It was then impossible to see a cable's length from the vessel, and in about twenty minutes more she struck with great violence on a reef of rocks running out from a creek right to the eastward bluff of Lambay Island. The shock was tremendous, shaking the vessel from stem to stern. She rose on the next wave, and drove in rather broadside on; and when she struck again still heaving, the sea made a clean breach over her amidships, setting everything on deck afloat. After two or three more shocks, the ship began to sink by the stern, and the scene of confusion and dismay that ensued baffles all description; the passengers rushing up the hatchway, husbands carrying their children, and women lying prostrate on the deck with their infants, screaming and imploring help."

Wooden spars and trunks were tossed about in the waves, and several of the crew immediately sprang onto the rocks and made their escape, some scaling vertiginous cliffs in search of help, a few staying put, attempting to help others ashore. An unfortunate few were sucked back under as they reached for those in trouble in an effort to help, the wind whipping at their sodden clothes and lashing their faces with spray, the pleas of the unlucky ringing in their ears.

They got a rope and a spar across, and saved many lives with this makeshift bridge before the waves pulled the *Tayleur* back off the rocks, allowing water to pour into its compartments, sinking it further, waves sweeping the decks of passengers and crew. Those who had been on the rope drowned or were smashed against the rocks, "the survivors on shore could perceive the unfortunate creatures, with their heads bruised and cut open, struggling amidst the waves, and one by one sinking under them." The screaming and pleas to God and those alive to save them were horrific to hear. So were the sudden silences as men, women, and children went under. This was a wet and pounding death.

"Among some of the earliest of the females who attempted to get on shore were some young Irishwomen. Most of them lost their hold of the rope, and fell into the sea." The clothing of the time, with its many layers, buttons, hooks and laces, weighed the women down in the water, and hindered them on the rope. Many of them would reach the halfway point on their way to the shore and freeze, fingers cold with sea spray, stiff and fumbling, till their grip faltered or a wave hit them – or others just as desperate for shore pushed them out of their way. Their skirts blooming around them, they vanished below the surface.

One of the more widely reported tragedies was that of the brave ship's surgeon, so optimistic of a safe and healthy voyage and a new life abroad with his family. Dr Cunningham did his best to calm those on deck, organising them for their escape, reassuring everyone he talked to. Some of the men who'd jumped onto the rocks had taken ropes with them, and he assisted with the rescue as waves broke over the deck, knocking the crowded passengers and crew over like skittles, then "struggled hard to save his wife and child, he had succeeded in getting about half–way to the shore on a rope holding his child by its clothes in his teeth, but just then the ship lurched outwards, by which the rope was dragged from the hands of those who held it on the lower rocks, and was held only by those above, thus running him high in the air, so that the brave fellow could not drop on the rock. Word was now given to lower the rope gently; but those who held it above let it go by the run, and the poor fellow, with his child, was buried in the waves; but in a short time he again appeared above the water, manfully battling with the waves and the portions of the wreck that now floated about him."

But he didn't give up, despite the loss of his infant son, Henry. "He at length swam to a ladder hanging by a rope alongside the ship, and got upon it. After he had been there a minute or two a woman floated close to him; he immediately took hold of her, and dragged her on the ladder, tenderly parted the hair from her face, and appeared to be encouraging her; but in another minute she was washed from his hold, and sank almost immediately. He then got up again into the ship and tried to get his wife on shore..." Holding his wife in his arms, he tried to carry her to safety but a wave washed them deep, and though he resurfaced, she was lost. Yet still, *still*, he continued to help. He could have reached the meagre ledge of shore, according to survivors who urged him on, but instead turned back when he noticed a woman panicking in the water, and tried to help her. She was so scared she tried to climb him in a frenzy and held him under till they both drowned. The water was becoming dense with debris and bodies.

"Every wave washed off scores at a time. We could see them struggle for a moment, then, tossing their arms, sink to rise no more. At length the whole of the ship sunk under water. There was a fearful struggle for a moment, and all, except two who were in the rigging, were gone. The coastguard, who had been appraised of the wreck, now came up; but all they could do was to attempt to save the two who were in the rigging. They managed to get a line to one of them, by fastening two lines, at the end of each of which was a piece of wood, to a single line, and guiding it from the rock to the spot where the poor fellow was, so that he could reach it. They then dragged him ashore. There was one fine young man [William Vivers, of Dumfries] left on the top, but they could not reach him, and when he saw them going away his cries were heartrending. About two o'clock the next morning the coastguard managed to reach him, after he had been in the top fourteen hours: you may fancy the poor fellow's joy at his deliverance." When they found him he was asleep, wrapped in a furl of sail tight against the wind.

Wrecks were common then, so common that when people on the Irish mainland spotted the *Tayleur* wrecking and sent word to the authorities, it was dismissed as confusion – as another ship, the *Scotland*, had wrecked nearby just 2 days before. Captain Dearl, who came to the rescue of the *Scotland* in his packet ship, the *Prince Arthur* – the equivalent to a post van now

110

– also came to the assistance of the survivors of the *Tayleur*, with food and drink and safe passage to Kingstown (now Dun Laoghaire).

The lucky ones were barely clothed, wet through, battered, bruised, and injured. Several had badly broken limbs and other wounds received as they sought to help those left in the water.

The Captain was among the last to leave the vessel as she sank, leaving Vivers and his companion swaying in the rigging above white tipped waves. He was one of a handful to complete the swim to shore, and nearly hadn't made it – but two passengers on witnessing his struggles reached out to pull him in and were themselves washed to the depths and drowned. He said "[I] could feel the dead bodies with [my] feet as [I] swam."

Out of 662 passengers, stowaways and crew, only 282 survived. Three women and three children made it to the cliff–face alive. One was the little baby, left wet and helpless on the deck by the waves.

The cliffs are near vertical for sixty feet, with no real beach, just a shelf dropping off into deeper water. Black rocks, sharp and rough to the touch, give way to lichen the rich yellow of egg yolk, tatters of grey, and clumps of springy green grass and pompoms of pinky–purple thrift. Seabirds scream and soar and defecate grey and white, and the waves sound more deadly the higher up you go. Brine hangs in the air, smelling of salt and the dark wreaths of seaweed tossed high onto the cliff face. How they climbed, shivering and injured, barefoot and desperate, up this hellish wall of rock with sodden shreds of clothes and babies strapped to their backs is amazing. Vivers and his companion could do nothing but cling ever tighter to the rigging, the ship now at rest on the seabed, the decks lost below the crashing grey waves, and watch them go.

The island was barely inhabited, with just a handful of homes and the lifeguard station, to which Captain Noble and the survivors proceeded once they'd got their breath back at the top of the cliff. The captain asked about for dry matches among the survivors on the rocks, but none were found, and his query gave rise to suspicions among the group that he had no idea of what land they were on. The lush green fields offered little shelter from the winds, and the islanders had little in terms of food and clothing to give the survivors. The waves and rocks had stripped them of most of their clothes and some of their skin – and all of their money. They rested in a hollow as the islanders worked together to help the ravaged victims of the sea. Food was provided by Mr Cusack, steward to the Lord of the island, Baron Talbot of Malahide.

One survivor told the papers: "The steward… threw open the house, which they call a castle, for us, as also did the coastguard. Here you would see some limping with their legs sprained, others without shoes or stockings – one with nothing but his shirt, the other with nothing but his trousers. The first day I had neither shoes nor stockings. We were served out with oatmeal and potatoes, and a pig was killed for us. We managed to make a good meal at the house of the coastguard man, at which we were stopping, and beds were made for us in all the rooms by spreading straw on the floor. We were almost starving. The night was dreadful, and we were many of us almost naked, wet through. In this state, we lay all night. The next day was worse than the day before…"

It took a gallant attempt by the boatmen of Rush to get clothing, spirits, and supplies to them as they shivered on the island, the filthy weather hampering all efforts to move them to the mainland.

Captain Dearl landed in the harbour on the other side of the island, and rushed hot coffee, bread, and mutton over to the wretched would–be emigrants, the rich scent of coffee overwhelming the sweet mustiness of the straw. Using what rags and clothing they had left, the survivors had bandaged wounded heads and sprained and broken limbs, making do until they saw doctors on the mainland. One enterprising lady had escaped the island with the fishing smack that had fought the waves to reach them, and made her way to Dublin to arrange help and practical assistance from the ship's insurers and representatives.

Most of the survivors were uninsured and penniless, everything they had of value lost beneath the crashing surf. They were also traumatised, shocked, and most had been bereaved. Some sat crying, others paced, asking if any had seen their family or friends. One man lost thirteen of his family; others lost wives and children, brothers and uncles, parents and servants. Whole families were wiped out, with distant relatives scouring the lists of survivors in the papers and waiting for further details as bodies and clothing were recovered from the water or washed up in bits on the Irish coast.

Fifty coffins were sent to the island. Boats sailed up and down for days, pulling bodies and body parts from the sea. Every pocket was searched, every embroidered initial noted with a description of the body to help with identification later. Often there were just partial remains left, heads and limbs dashed off by the rocks, clothes and skin scoured by barnacles and nibbled by fish, so only crimson torsos remained.

The last body to be found washed up towards the end of summer, seven months later, with just the waistband of trousers still binding its middle. But the repercussions weren't over by then. Not by a longshot.

88 people took the replacement voyage offered as recompense and emigrated to Australia within the year. Some returned home, penniless, to families who'd either said their final goodbyes or waited to be sent for once gold was struck.

Four inquiries followed, using the bodies of little Henry Cunningham, the doctor's son, and Edward Kaley, second mate, as specimen cases. Most of the bodies were mangled or lost, or jammed in crevices in the rocks and too difficult to immediately retrieve. These two were well known among the surviving passengers and crew and therefore identifiable, and just in case there was a problem with either of them, a third body was stored for viewing by the jury.

It was the nameless body of a ten year—old boy with a wooden leg. They believed that such an unusual feature would allow his name to be supplied by survivors, relatives or neighbours in a short space of time. He endured an amputation in the mid—19th century, before antibiotics or effective anaesthetic were available, then prepared for the long voyage to Australia. To then perish after less than two days at sea seems monstrously unfair.

The first inquiry, in the Grand Hotel at Malahide, called several survivors as witness — and smacks of a cover—up. A Mr Jones, an underwriter from Liverpool, was there supposedly out of mere curiosity rather than to represent the company — nobody attended for that. But when Captain Noble was called for, he'd left in a carriage with the first mate. The magistrates were furious, sending for him as a matter of urgency. Someone had witnessed Jones taking Noble to one side beforehand and having an animated conversation with him before his hasty exit, the mate leaving his glass of ale half drunk on the bar as he followed him. A Mr Walker said: "Mr Coroner, the captain was here in this room a few moments since, and he was called out of it by that gentleman (pointing to Mr Jones)... and he has not since returned."

When a carefully—spoken Noble returned and took the stand, he defended White Star's honour and claimed it was *he* who had persuaded the owners to let the ship sail before she was ready. There was a lot of suspicion cast on this and his statement regarding his supposed confidence and happiness with the actions and competence of his crew, but he would not speak against his employers even when several credible witnesses cast doubt on his version of events. He acknowledged his mistakes in not testing the compasses or sounding the lead, saying "I made no experiment down the river, and was ignorant of the sailing qualities of the ship. I supposed, as is customary, that she would have answered her helm". His coolness, bravery, and actions during the wrecking were recognised in the inquiry and somewhat begrudgingly in the papers over the following months.

Despite Jones' and Noble's best efforts, the jury soon returned the verdict: "the parties were drowned by the sinking of the said ship off Lambay Island, and that this deplorable accident occurred in consequence of the highly culpable neglect of the owners, in permitting the vessel to leave port without compasses properly adjusted, or a sufficient trial having taken place to learn whether she was under the control of her helm or not, and we find that Captain Noble did not take sufficient precaution to insure the safety of the vessel by rounding to after he found the compasses were in error, but we consider, from the time the vessel came in sight of land, that he acted with coolness and courage, and used every exertion in his power to save the lives of the passengers."

Castigated in the press, he kept his certificate – allowing him to continue captaining the emigrant ships. But his career came at the cost of his marriage and good health. Another ship he captained was lost at sea, his wife ran off to London with a travelling salesman, and he died a broken man at 36.

As for the so-called Ocean Child, as the papers christened the nameless orphan, at first he was believed to be little Henry Cunningham, the doctor's son. Nobody laid claim to him, and with thirteen babies and their families dead in the wreck, there was little chance of identifying him from paperwork alone.

He was taken to 22 Herbert Place, Dublin – the home of Reverend John H. Armstrong and his young family – newspapers both national and local covering the story of the wreck and the child across the UK, donations and offers to foster him pouring in from the rich, the poor, and all manner of people in between.

The Rev John Armstrong was Chaplain of St Stephen's Church, just a few yards from his terraced house. He was born about 1819 in Dublin, and attended the well-respected Trinity College there before travelling round the Holy Land, Athens, Rome, and other capital cities of Europe. Orphaned at about the same age as little Arthur, he was raised by his uncle and was a cultured, educated, generous man. He and his wife, Isabella Jane, lived in the four storey house overlooking the canal with their 4 year old, Francis, and welcomed the ten month old orphan into their home as they set about tracing his relatives.

A month later, he had a name – Arthur Charles Griffiths – and a grandmother coming to take him home. They left Ireland on the 9am boat home on Wednesday February 22nd, she cradling his little body in her arms as they boarded the vessel, and returned to Herefordshire. The Rev John Jebb, a Dubliner living in Peterstow not far from Arthur's new home in the village of Ross, kept an eye on the little boy and maintained correspondence with his former foster father. Arthur's family was poor, but the subscriptions meant he would want for nothing material – and that a doctor would attend when he grew ill.

Child mortality was high then, generally the ones who made it five would survive to adulthood. Arthur had been through a lot, what with the travel to the *Tayleur*, the near-drowning, and then the journey home.

It was a comparatively mild spring, a time of snowdrops then daffodils and lambs bouncing through fields, birds singing and showing off, and leaves just starting to green the trees. Arthur lived through his first birthday on Friday 24th March, and survived another five days, before dying of dysentery at his aunt's house in Ross on the Wednesday, just two months after the wrecking of the *Tayleur*.

The 'bloody flux' as it was often known killed more young men than warfare at that time, and in children it started with nausea, fever, abdominal cramps, vomiting, and diarrhoea which could happen as often as hourly with blood, pus, and mucus expelled amongst it. This coupled with the vomiting could lead to severe dehydration very quickly, and result in shock, and death. The child may be in terrible pain but too low on fluids to cry proper tears. Rev Jebb buried him on Saturday afternoon, April 1st, in Peterstow graveyard, and the sad news was broken to the interested public by Rev Armstrong in a letter to the papers.

"It is with much sorrow that I have to announce… that the life so wondrously preserved has just been closed. I have this morning received a letter from the Rev John Jebb, who has anxiously watched over the child since he left my house, informing me that yesterday the little fellow sank under a chronic intestinal disorder… He is now in better hands…"

There is no gravestone, no marker or memorial for this little lost boy. None but the blank stones where he lost his parents, spattered with pale corals not lichen, and attended by rust bottomed lobsters. Real fortunes stitched into long rotted corsets and clothing are somewhere beneath the fools' gold and counterfeit coins, divers sometimes brave the cold Irish waters there, visiting with flippers and cameras, hoping for an interesting picture or the glint of bullion. The long bodies of anemones sway with the tide in hungry bouquets, snatching at plankton as seals bob and dive over the last remains of the *Tayleur*, and the only sound there now comes from the crash of the waves and the screaming of the gulls.

ACKNOWLEDGEMENTS

With thanks to:

Amy Burns of **Spilling Ink Review** for publishing *Acceptance, Firework Sand*, and *Black Fish*

Susan Tepper of **Wilderness House Literary Review** for publishing *The Rescue*

Cheryl Anne Gardner of **Apocrypha & Abstractions** for publishing *Imago*

Thomas Pluck, Fiona Johnson, and Ron Earl Phillips of **The Lost Children Charity Anthology** for publishing *The premature ending of Annie MacLeod*

Patti Nase of **pattinase.blogspot.com** for publishing *The Creature in the Coal*

Craig Sherwood of Warrington Museum for his expert assistance with research for *An Unusual Darkness* and *Prospects*

Win Robinson of Herefordshire Archive Service for her time and assistance with research for *Prospects*

and Matt Potter of **Pure Slush**

Previously published

Firework sand ★ – *September 2011*
Acceptance – *March 2011*
Black Fish ★★ – *April 2011*
Spilling Ink Review
http://spillinginkreview.com/
★ *Honourable Mention – 2011 Spilling Ink Short Story Prize*
★★ *1st Prize, 2011 Spilling Ink Nonfiction Competition*

The Rescue – *January 2012*
Wilderness House Literary Review
http://www.whlreview.com/

Snow Go – *August 2011*
Miss – *September 2011*
Yellow – *November 2011*
Slut's Pennies ('slut' print anthology) – *November 2011*
Protein – *December 2011*
Pure Slush
http://pureslush.webs.com/

Imago – *November 2011*
Apocrypha and Abstractions
http://apocryphaandabstractions.wordpress.com/

The premature ending of Annie MacLeod – *November 2011*
Lost Children: A Charity Anthology
http://the–lost–children.blogspot.com.au/

The Creature in the Coal – *October 2011*
Patti Nase's blog
http://pattinase.blogspot.com.au/

About the Author

Gill Hoffs lives with her family and an ever–dwindling supply of Nutella in the North of England. She reads and writes about a number of subjects and genres, including maritime history, thrillers, ghost stories and the supernatural, unusual adventures, and occasionally children's books, too.

Gill's work has won several international competitions and is widely available online and in print. Gill's second novel, *In her skin*, the first in a series of crime thrillers set in Warrington in the north of England, was recommended for shortlisting for the 2011 Virginia Prize.

Writing with her cat by her feet and snacks close at hand, Gill relishes research and alliteration, and stands in the sea at night in her wellington boots, writing, whenever she can arrange it.

Find her online at http://gillhoffs.wordpress.com/

Other books from *Pure Slush*

Visit the *Pure Slush* Store online:
http://pureslush.webs.com/store.htm

Many Fish to Fry
by Abha Iyengar
ISBN: 978-1-925101-59-1

The Company of Men
by Luisa Brenta
ISBN: 978-1-925101-06-5

The Vixen Scream
by Nancy Stohlman
ISBN: 978-1-925101-11-9

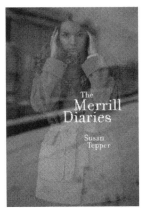

The Merrill Diaries
by Susan Tepper
ISBN: 978-0-9922778-2-6

itch
by Gary Percesepe
ISBN: 978-1-925101-21-8

Hard
by Dusty-Anne Rhodes
ISBN: 978-1-925101-80-5

Printed in Great Britain
by Amazon